T0171712

THE COLLECTED WORKS OF W. B. YEATS
Richard J. Finneran and George Mills Harper
General Editors

VOLUME I: *The Poems,*
ed. Richard J. Finneran

VOLUME II: *The Plays,*
ed. David R. Clark

VOLUME III: *Autobiographies,*
ed. Douglas Archibald, J. Fraser Cocks III,
and Gretchen L. Schwenker

VOLUME IV: *Early Essays,*
ed. Warwick Gould and Deirdre Toomey

VOLUME V: *Later Essays,*
ed. William H. O'Donnell

VOLUME VI: *Prefaces and Introductions,*
ed. William H. O'Donnell

VOLUME VII: *Letters to the New Island,*
ed. George Bornstein and Hugh Witemeyer

VOLUME VIII: *The Irish Dramatic Movement,*
ed. Mary FitzGerald

VOLUME IX: *Early Articles and Reviews,*
ed. John P. Frayne

VOLUME X: *Later Articles and Reviews,*
ed. Colton Johnson

VOLUME XI: *Mythologies,*
ed. Warwick Gould, Phillip L. Marcus,
and Michael Sidnell

VOLUME XII: *John Sherman and Dhoya,*
ed. Richard J. Finneran

VOLUME XIII: *A Vision* (1925),
ed. Connie K. Hood and Walter Kelly Hood

VOLUME XIV: *A Vision* (1937),
ed. Connie K. Hood and Walter Kelly Hood

THE COLLECTED WORKS OF W. B. YEATS
VOLUME XII

W. B. YEATS

John Sherman

AND

Dhoya

EDITED BY

Richard J. Finneran

Macmillan Publishing Company

NEW YORK

Macmillan Publishing Company
866 Third Avenue
New York, NY 10022

Macmillan Publishing Company is part of the
Maxwell Communication Group of Companies.

Library of Congress Cataloging-in-Publication Data
(Revised for v. 12)

Yeats, W. B. (William Butler), 1865–1939.
  The collected works of W. B. Yeats.
  Includes bibliographical references and indexes.
  v. 1. The poems / edited by Richard J. Finneran — v. 6. Pref-
aces and introductions / edited by William H. O'Donnell —
[etc.] — v. 12. John Sherman and Dhoya / edited by Richard J.
Finneran.
  I. Finneran, Richard J. II. Harper, George Mills.
III. Title.
PR5900.A2F56 1989   821'.8   88-27365
ISBN 978-1-4516-4645-0

Macmillan books are available at special discounts for bulk
purchases for sales promotions, premiums, fund-raising, or
educational use. For details, contact:

Special Sales Director
Macmillan Publishing Company
866 Third Avenue
New York, NY 10022

10 9 8 7 6 5 4 3 2 1

Printed in the United States of America

CONTENTS

FOREWORD

This volume represents my third attempt to edit William Butler Yeats's *John Sherman and Dhoya*. The first was begun as a dissertation at the University of North Carolina at Chapel Hill in 1967; it was completed the following year, directed by Richard Harter Fogle. My second was a slightly revised version of that dissertation, published in 1969 by the Wayne State University Press in Detroit, Michigan. Although the present volume does not include a collation of the textual variants between the 1891 and the 1908 editions, as did the first two attempts, in all other respects it supersedes them.

Returning to the same text after two decades has proven to be an interesting if often humbling experience. Happily, I did not discover any significant errors in the reading text of *John Sherman and Dhoya* published in 1969, but much else has required refinement. For instance, trusting to the authority of Allan Wade's *A Bibliography of the Writings of W. B. Yeats*, I repeated his citation of three English "editions" of the work in 1891–92, whereas I now offer a different story. Trusting equally to the authority of Joseph Hone's biography, I repeated the information that Yeats earned £40 for the work, whereas I now think the true sum perhaps no more than half that amount. Either believing in the existence of a "common body of knowledge" or else simply not thinking very clearly, I passed over in silence numerous allusions large and small; whereas I now annotate virtually all direct references (for better or for worse). And, of course, I have benefited from two decades of Yeats scholarship, particularly from William M. Murphy's essay on the autobiographical level of *John Sherman* and from the new material offered in volume one of the *Collected Letters*.

To modify slightly a remark by Yeats, it is indeed true that "all editing is collaboration." To those whose assistance was acknowledged in the 1969 edition, I should like to add the following: Robert Bearman (The Shakespeare Birthplace Trust); George Bornstein; Allen W. Bosch (Kenyon College Library); William R. Cagle (The Lilly Library, Indiana University); Wayne Chapman; the late Ian Fletcher; Vincent Giroud and Patricia C. Willis (The Beinecke Rare Book and Manuscript Library, Yale University); Bruce Harkness; Elizabeth Heine; Virginia Hyde; Christina Hunt Mahony; Laura Morland; Stephen Parrish; Lawrence Rainey; Carla Rickerson (University of Washington Library); Ronald Schuchard; Peter Shillingsburg; and Colin Smythe.

One person mentioned in 1969 I cite again, not only because of his continuing assistance to all my work over the past two decades, this edition included, but also because his death in Berkeley, California, on 16 March 1991 was a deep personal loss: Brendan O Hehir.

Finally, I rededicate this edition to Maude Florence Finneran.

Mandeville, Louisiana
6 April 1991

EDITOR'S INTRODUCTION

On 13 August 1887, W. B. Yeats informed a correspondent that he was "resolved to try story writing but
so far have not made a start."[1] At the age of twenty-
two, he was already an established writer in the country
of his birth, contributing both poems and critical essays
to several Irish periodicals. A week before announcing
his new resolve, he had achieved his first publication in
America, a poem in *The Boston Pilot*. In September he
would introduce himself to English readers, with a lyric
in *The Leisure Hour*. The short story must now have
seemed a fitting genre to essay. Quickly fulfilling his
promise, Yeats was able to announce on 10 September
that he had written "a short romance of ancient
Ireland—somewhat over dreamy and florid but quite
readible* any way and now commence another of latter
day Ireland" (CL1 36).

Almost thirty years later, he would recall his entrance
into fiction as motivated by his father, John Butler Yeats,
who was concerned that the state of the family finances
might deflect his eldest son into a career as a journalist:

> I was greatly troubled because I was making no
> money. . . . Our neighbour, York Powell, at last of-
> fered to recommend me for the sub-editorship of, I
> think, [the] Manchester Courier. I took some days to
> think it over; it meant an immediate income, but it

---

* *The Collected Letters* is faithful to Yeats's erratic spelling.

was a Unionist paper. At last I told my father that I could not accept and he said 'You have taken a great weight off my mind.' My father suggested that I should write a story and, partly in London and partly in Sligo, where I stayed with my uncle George Pollexfen, I wrote Dhoya, a fantastic tale of the heroic age. My father was dissatisfied and said he meant a story with real people, and I began John Sherman, putting into it my memory of Sligo and my longing for it.[2]

This account may not be entirely accurate—*Dhoya* was apparently written entirely in Sligo—but financial considerations were doubtless a factor in Yeats's turn to fiction.

Having completed *Dhoya*, Yeats seems to have set it aside for several months, until on 13 December 1887 he submitted it for publication in *The Gael*, "hoping it may suit for the Xmas number for some number anyway. . . ." (CL1 43). Since no complete file of *The Gael* is known to survive, it is impossible to say if *Dhoya* was published there, but it seems unlikely.[3] It would be another two and a half years before the story is mentioned in the extant correspondence.

By beginning his career in fiction with "a fantastic tale of the heroic age," Yeats was being true to both his aesthetic and his nationalistic principles. Indeed, in his first critical article, published less than a year before the composition of *Dhoya*, he had argued that

Of all the many things the past bequeaths to the future, the greatest are great legends; they are the mother of nations. I hold it the duty of every Irish reader to study those of his own country till they are familiar as his own hands, for in them is the Celtic heart.[4]

Or, as he would shortly inform his American readers, "Cosmopolitan literature is, at best, but a poor bubble": "there is no fine nationality without literature, . . . no fine literature without nationality."[5]

Yeats thus bases *Dhoya* on a common motif in Irish literature, a liaison between a mortal and a fairy. Indeed, while writing the story he was also working on "The Wanderings of Oisin," a long narrative poem employing the same motif. Moreover, although *Dhoya* is a mythological tale, set in "those mysterious pre-human ages when life lasted for hundreds of years" (LNI 80), Yeats presents it as a living legend in the West of Ireland. He would, of course, have known of "a good anchorage called Pooldoy" in Sligo Bay,[6] and he took a special delight in discovering a continuity of belief in legendary materials. Writing to Katharine Tynan shortly after completing *Dhoya*, for instance, he explained that "I went last Wednesday up Ben Bulban to see the place where Dermot died, a dark pool fabulously deep and still haunted—1732 feet above the sea line, open to all winds. . . . All peasents at the foot of the mountain know the legend, and know that Dermot still haunts the pool, and fear it. Every hill and stream is some way or other connected with the story" (CL1 37). But perhaps Yeats's most cogent explanation of his goal in stories such as *Dhoya* was offered to readers of *The Gael* just a few months before he set to work in fiction:

Under all the old legends there is, without doubt,

much fact, though, I confess, I care but little whether there be or not. A nation's history is not in what it does, this invader or that other; the elements or destiny decides all that; but what a nation imagines that is its history, there is its heart; than its legends, a nation owns nothing more precious. Without her possible mythical siege of Troy, perhaps, Greece would never have had her real Thermopylae. Learn those of your own country, let the young love them.[7]

Thus, *Dhoya* was altogether in accord with Yeats's literary ideals in the formative years of his career; and as matters developed, it was to serve as the inspiration for much of his later effort in prose fiction.

However, Yeats next turned away from Irish mythology and folklore as materials for his fiction: as he had promised in his letter of 10 September 1887, having finished *Dhoya*, he would now "commence another of latter day Ireland" (CL1 36). Apparently he delayed this project for several months. On 12 February 1888 he wrote Tynan that "soon" he would "set to work at a short romance," mentioning that he was following his father's wishes in the matter (CL1 59). A month later he was still promising to "begin an Irish story, I do not believe in it, but may do for some Irish paper, and give me practice" (CL1 57). Another month passed, and Yeats was "reading up for my romance," which was then to have an eighteenth-century setting: "I should dream of it only I do not dream much. I am very cheerful over it. Making my romance I have so much affirmative in me . . ." (CL1 59).

At last, by early May 1888 Yeats was able to tell Tynan that he was "absorbed" in the composition of what would become *John Sherman*, apparently already transposed to a contemporary setting: "I also am writing a short story—it goes on fairly well the style quite sane and the theme modern, more character than plot in it" (CL1 67). By the middle of the month he had shown a draft to a friend and could offer further details: "My story goes well the plot is laid mainly in Sligo. It deels more with charecter than incidents. Sparling praised it much thinks my skill lies more in charecter than incidents." He also noted that "my father was very anxious for me to go on with my story . . ." (CL1 69–70). By the middle of June the work was almost completed, but Yeats was not optimistic about its prospects:

> my father . . . does not wish me to do critical work. He wants me to write stories. I am working at one as you know. It is almost done now. Their is some good charecter drawing I think, but the construction is patchy and incoherent. I have not much hope of it. It will join I fear my ever multiplying boxes of unsaleable MSS—work to[o] strange at one moment and to[o] incoherent the next for any first class Magazine and too ambitious for local papers. Yet I dont know that it is ambition for I have no wish but to write a saleable story. (CL1 71)

However, a few days later Yeats was more enthusiastic about *John Sherman*: "My story is going well another chapter will finish it. It is rather a curious production for me—full of observation and worldly wisdom or what pretends to be such" (CL1 75).

Around this time Yeats seems to have suspended work on *John Sherman*, telling Tynan on 28 July 1888

that "My story waits for its last chapter and will have
to wait until immediate work concludes" (CL1 88). It
is not until late September that he took it up again. By
8 October a draft had been finished. He wrote John
O'Leary that "My novel or novelette draws to a close.
The first draft is complete. It is all about a curate and a
young man from the country. The difficulty is to keep
the characters from turning into eastern symbolic mon-
sters of some sort which would be a curious thing to
happen to a curate and a young man from the country"
(CL1 104).[8] On 14 November he described the work as
"a very quiet plotless little story" but noted that a friend
had made suggestions for revision:

> on reading my story to Edwin Ellis Saturday week
> he suggested alterations of much importance on
> which I am still at work and it is quite needful for
> me to get this story in some editors hands at once as
> we have not been doing very well lately. I think how-
> ever three days will quite finish it. . . . (CL1 106)

Yeats appears to have overestimated the speed with
which he could revise *John Sherman*, but by 4 December
1888 the novelette had been completed. He informed
Tynan that "my practice over 'Sherman' has made my
prose come much more easily. I am now setting to work
on an article on Todhunters book" (CL1 110).

Despite his anxiety over the family finances, Yeats
seems to have made no immediate attempt to have *John
Sherman* published. On 21 April 1889 he explained to
Tynan: "I know I gained greatly from my experiment
in novel writing. The hero turned out a bad character
and so I did not try to sell the story any where. I am in
hopes he may reform" (CL1 162). Almost eighteen

months passed before he would inform Tynan on 6 October 1890 that "I have retouched my Story John Sherman & am trying to get it published. Edward Garnett, author of the Paradox Club, is going to read it & see if it will suit the publisher he reads for *ie* Fisher Unwin" (CL1 230). Garnett apparently did not take up this task at once, though, as it is not until 5 March 1891 that Yeats passed on the news that Garnett was "quite enthusiastic" about *John Sherman* (CL1 245). Although Yeats may have first offered the story to William Heinemann, in late March of 1891 he happily wrote Tynan that "My 'John Sherman' has at last been taken by Fisher Unwin for his Pseudonm Library," adding "I am to get a royalty but not until it gets into its second thousand if it ever do so" (CL1 247).

Yeats was glad to have a contract but frustrated that his work would be published anonymously: "Unwin I believe makes rather a point of the Pseudonimous nature of the books," he told O'Leary (CL1 248). This lack of publicity would be less than helpful to a young writer still seeking to make a name for himself. Indeed, he had boasted to Tynan that being able to include the novelette in his bibliography for 1891 would place him "well in evidence" (CL1 245).

In the event, though, Yeats acquiesced to the wishes of his publisher. He chose as a pseudonym "Ganconagh," the name of an Irish fairy, and composed an "Apology" to explain this persona. But the problem of anonymous publication may well have been one of Yeats's reasons for adding to the volume *Dhoya*, an expansion we first hear of (under an earlier title) in late June 1891:

My novel has gone to press but does not come out

until September. I have sent in with it, to be put in the same volume, a short tale of ancient Irish legendary days and called the book *John Sherman and The Midnight Ride.* The second part of the title refers to the second story. My pseudonym is Ganconagh, the name of an Irish spirit. (CL1 250–51)[9]

The short story included (or perhaps Yeats now added to it) a lyric already published as "Girl's Song" in *The Wanderings of Oisin and Other Poems* (1889). Thus, as he told Tynan, "the incognito will be pretty transparent" (CL1 253). Indeed, Yeats made a point of telling potential reviewers of *John Sherman and Dhoya* that the text offered a ready key to disclose his identity, even supplying at least one of them with the precise reference: "I want it to be known as mine—the poem at page 187 is in my book of poems so the disguise is not very deep . . ." (CL1 268). There may well have been other reasons for the addition of the short story—Yeats (or Unwin) may have wanted a longer book; *Dhoya* was a completed story awaiting a publisher, and moreover one which firmly shows Yeats's commitment to Irish literature rather than English; and so on. But Yeats's desire to expand his acknowledged canon may have been foremost: indeed, when *The Celtic Twilight* was published in 1893, *John Sherman and Dhoya* was included in the list of books "By the same Author."

With the book in press in July 1891, Yeats expressed to Tynan his concern for its reception and began to do what he could to stimulate favorable reviews:

I am rather anxious about "Sherman". It is good I believe but it will be a toss up how the reviewers take

it—for if they look for the ordinary stuff of novels
they will find nothing. Do what you can for it—for
a success with stories would solve many problems
with me & I write them easily. (CL1 256–57)

Two similar letters survive. As they provide Yeats's
most extended commentary on *John Sherman and Dhoya*,
they are of particular interest. First, to Father Matthew
Russell early in November 1891:

> I send you a copy of my novel "John Sherman". If
> you will kindly review it & say that it is mine I shall
> be well pleased. People are given to thinking I can
> only write of the fantastical & wild & this book has
> to do so far as the long story is concerned with very
> ordinary persons & events. . . . I shall probably write
> other stories but of a more dramatic & stirring kind
> if this goes at all well. Dowden quotes "Sherman" in
> the "Fortnightly" by the by. He told me he likes the
> story that "it is full of beautiful things" and "very
> interesting" though not a strong and dramatic story
> in any way nor of course was it so intended. The
> American edition has been sold & success seems
> likely. (CL1 268)[10]

Finally, to Tynan again, on 2 December offering a de-
fense of the novelette as an "Irish" work:

> I studied my characters in Ireland & described a typical
> Irish feeling in Sherman's devotion to Ballah. A West
> of Ireland feeling I might almost say for like that of
> Allingham for Ballyshannon it is local rather than
> national. Sherman belonged like Allingham to the

small gentry who in the West at any rate love their native places without perhaps loving Ireland. They do not travell & are shut off from England by the whole breadth of Ireland with the result that they are forced to make their native town their world. I remember when we were children how intense our devotion was to all things in Sligo & still see in my mother the old feeling. I claim for this & other reasons that Sherman is as much an Irish novel as anything by Banim or Griffen. Lady Wylde has written me an absurd & enthusiastic letter about it. She is queer enough to prefer it to my poems. (CL1 274–75)[11]

The exact circumstances of the printing and publication of *John Sherman and Dhoya* are less than fully clear. Yeats had the volume in hand no later than 1 September 1891, as on that day he inscribed a copy to Maud Gonne.[12] Lily Yeats's copy (now in the Library of Trinity College Dublin) is also dated "Sep. 1891," and on the fourth of that month Yeats informed William Ernest Henley that "Unwin will send you in a day or two a story of mine called *John Sherman*. There is a little thing bound up with it called *Dhoya* that may please you" (CL1 264). But *John Sherman and Dhoya* was not officially published until the second week of November 1891, a copy being received at the British Library on Friday the thirteenth.[13] However, that copy was of the "second edition." Moreover, at least two of the volumes which Yeats sent to reviewers on 9 November 1891 (CL1 270) were of the "second edition."[14] It thus seems virtually certain that, as was to happen with *The Wind Among the Reeds* a few years later, the two "editions" were printed simultaneously, the only difference being the cover and title page.

It is therefore rather likely that the accepted figure of 2,000 copies for the first edition (1,644 paper, 356 cloth) may well encompass at least both the first and second "editions."[15] This possibility complicates the question of Yeats's profits from *John Sherman and Dhoya*. Just before the book was published, Yeats told O'Leary that "Garnett says £30 probably which will be very good indeed for a first story" (CL1 269). On 28 November he received £10 for the American edition, his only documented income (CL1 274, 276). On 1 May 1892 he asked Unwin to "get the clerk to find out what may be due to me for 'John Sherman & Dhoya' & send me the amount some time this week" (CL1 294). Unwin obviously did not respond, as Yeats wrote again on 23 August: "There are I beleive a few pounds still due to me as royalties for 'John Sherman' at least so I heard when I received the £10 for the American edition. It would be very convenient if you could send them to me now" (CL1 309). At some point in 1892, Unwin issued a third "edition," perhaps in conjunction with his publication of *The Countess Kathleen and Various Legends and Lyrics* in September. Yeats makes no mention of this "edition" in the extant correspondence, and it is likely to have consisted of a small number of copies.[16]

Thus, Joseph Hone's claim in his authorized biography of Yeats that *John Sherman and Dhoya* "earned £40 for the author" seems rather high.[17] In any case, Yeats was concerned not only with his finances but also with the reviews: these might best be described as mixed but on the whole favorable. The earliest notice of the dozen which have so far been traced was also one of the most negative. Yeats was presumably amused to find that "L.F.A." of the *Illustrated London News* for 12 November 1891 concluded that "the author . . . is evidently a lady," but he was probably less delighted with the review as a whole, which ignores *Dhoya* and offers the following suggestion:

> . . . I entreat Mr. Unwin to impress upon this pseudonymous lady that even a jilt who throws herself into the arms of a curate may perform that astonishing feat without accessories which would certainly startle most of the curates with whom I have the honor to be acquainted. (p. 667)

However, on 24 November 1891 an anonymous reviewer in the Manchester *Guardian* was rather more favorable. The volume was adjudged a "good addition" to the Pseudonym Library, and *John Sherman* was found to show "very considerable talent": "The story is nothing; the telling a good deal" (p. 7).[18] An anonymous critic in the *Athenaeum* (26 December 1891) was less impressed, arguing that *Dhoya* "has a vague charm of atmosphere, but little else that a reader can seize upon," while *John Sherman* exhibited "a certain grace of style which atones in part for the extreme thinness of . . . matter" (p. 859).

Perhaps the most complimentary review of *John Sherman and Dhoya* was published anonymously in the prestigious *Saturday Review of Literature* (5 December 1891):

> *John Sherman and Dhoya,* by "Ganconagh" (Fisher Unwin), must charm all who appreciate artistic work

that is delicate, unobtrusive, and intuitive. Of material that has been a thousand times employed in fiction, and often grievously marred in the using, the author of *John Sherman* has called forth a new heaven and a new earth—"Ganconagh," in brief, has the creative faculty and the imagination that vitalizes the gift. Each of the four chief characters in this short story is in its way an excellent study after nature. Clever as *John Sherman* is, cleverness seems almost an odious quality to ascribe to pathos so unassertive, humour so delicate, and observation so penetrative. To "tell" the story by way of abstract or paraphrase would be an offence to the artistic conscience, and at best could convey little or nothing of its peculiar charm. *Dhoya* is not a story, and is far slighter. It is an Irish legend, or apologue, of the days when there were giants in the land, and fairies, and magical influences. If there are any admirers of *Ossian* that yet remain among us, we would ask them to read *Dhoya*, and perpend thereupon. (p. 650)

It is easy enough to understand why it was an extract from this review that was used as a blurb for *John Sherman and Dhoya* when it was advertised in *The Celtic Twilight*.

Another very favorable English assessment was the last to appear, in the *Westminster Review* for February 1892:

. . . the first story, *John Sherman*, is not at all like the ordinary run of fiction, either in its incidents or its characters, and it maintains throughout a pleasant subdued interest. *Dhoya* is a wild imaginative legend of a fiercely raging Irish giant. . . . His sad story is very skilfully told; the treatment and the accessories are large and heroic; there is none of that *mièvrerie* which often mars such attempts, jarring, in its modern sentimentalism, like a false note. (p. 225)

As might be expected, the Irish reviewers were consistently positive; thanks to Yeats's campaign, they were also aware of the identity of the author. An anonymous critic in *United Ireland* for 28 November 1891 went so far as to compare Yeats with the continental masters, finding in *John Sherman* a style "quiet, and admirably restrained":

The story of John Sherman is slight. There is not much power in it, and not much plot. But Mr. Yeats has fashioned his style after the serious Russian model, and holds his reader. . . . Mr. Yeats has succeeded in producing a book to some extent unique in English literature; not, all the same, let us say, a brilliant book, nor a very remarkable one, but a book displaying very great possibilities in the author.

But the reviewer was even more impressed with *Dhoya*, correctly predicting that it would be the model for Yeats's further efforts in fiction:

The story of Dhoya is a delightful love tale, and Mr. Yeats tells it with true poetic instinct. This is much the better performance of the two; indeed, we have no hesitation in saying that 'Dhoya' runs a very good chance of becoming literature. . . . [L]egendary tales of this kind are much more in Mr. Yeats' line than 'John Sherman.' (p. 5)

Writing in the *Irish Monthly* (December 1891), Father Matthew Russell followed Yeats's wishes in his letter of early November 1891, not only identifying the author but also noting that "it is an additional surprise to find that this novel does not deal with anything wild or fantastical, but is a pleasant narrative touching of ordinary persons and events. . . . The descriptions both of scenery and character are full of quaint little touches of very subtle observation. The style is perhaps most remarkable for a dainty simplicity, lit up now and then by a striking thought and even a brilliant aphorism" (pp. 662–63). Tynan likewise complied with Yeats's petition that she describe *John Sherman* as "Irish," reviewing the work anonymously in both the *Dublin Evening Telegraph* (29 December 1891) and the *Irish Daily Independent* (4 January 1892), noting in the first that "Mr. Yeats in creating 'John Sherman' has shown us a type Irish and pathetic which none of our other novelists has hit upon. Where in all the world but Ireland would you find John Sherman . . . ?" (p. 2).

In light of the reviews, then, the "London correspondent" for *United Ireland* was surely correct when he wrote in the issue for 23 January 1892 that "Mr. Yeats' recent book in the Pseudonym Library—'John Sherman and Dhoya'—has greatly raised his already high reputation, and is selling very well . . ." (p. 5). Yeats had told Father Russell that "I shall probably write other stories but of a more dramatic & stirring kind if this goes at all well" (CL1 268), and the reviews and sales alone might have been encouragement enough. But William Ernest Henley, editor of the *National Observer*, provided a crucial incentive. Yeats told AE on 20 November 1891 that "Henley has written to me about 'Sherman & Dhoya'. He likes them very much but likes Doya best" (CL1 271). Within a few days he could inform O'Leary that the *National Observer* "have asked me, by the by for stories like Dhoya if I can make them short enough to fit their pages. I doubt it can be done but mean to try" (CL1 272). Yeats not only tried but succeeded. Beginning in November 1892, Yeats would publish in Henley's *National Observer* and, later, *New Review* well over half of the stories which were to comprise *The Secret Rose* (1897), his single most important collection of fiction. Yeats's decision to include *Dhoya* with *John Sherman*, then, was to play an important role in the shape of his career in the 1890s. As the *United Ireland* reviewer had noted, *Dhoya* was "much more in Mr. Yeats's line," and in the event it became the progenitor of the bulk of his published fiction.

If in *Dhoya* Yeats had turned to Irish mythology, for *John Sherman* he looked rather closer to home. As he informed Tynan on 5 March 1891, "There is more of myself in it than any thing I have done" (CL1 245–46). In the fullest study of the autobiographical level of the novelette, William M. Murphy has cogently argued that "One begins to suspect that if one only knew even more about the daily life of the Yeatses, one could assign to every person, object, and incident in the novel a corresponding equivalent in [Yeats's] own life."[19] Though none of the characters is a mimetic representation of a particular individual, it is clear that Sherman is based primarily on Yeats himself, with some aspects of his cousin Henry Middleton. Howard draws extensively on the Reverend John Dowden, brother of Edward. Moreover, the relationship between Sherman and Howard adumbrates Yeats's theory of the divided self, what he would later describe with such terms as the Self versus the Anti-Self. Margaret derives from Laura Armstrong, also the model for Vivien in an early play which Yeats never published. Tynan is surely the primary source for Mary Carton.

Even the minor characters have their real-life counterparts. For instance, at the end of the First Part of *John Sherman*, Sherman describes "a very dirty old woman sitting by a crate of geese" on the steamer to Liverpool, who criticizes him for abandoning Sligo for London. Yeats has combined a remark made by his aunt Agnes Pollexfen with another childhood memory:

> When I was a little boy, an old woman who had come to Liverpool with crates of fowl made me miserable by throwing her arms around me, the moment I had alighted from my cab, and telling the sailor who carried my luggage that she had held me in her arms when I was a baby.[20]

Not only the characters but also the themes of *John Sherman* have their analogues in Yeats's own thought. Yeats told O'Leary that the "motif" of the work was "hatred of London" (CL1 110), and Sherman's attitude toward the English capital is parallel to Yeats's. Writing to Tynan on 25 August 1888, Yeats noted that he would "get back to my story in which I pour out all my grievances against this meloncholy London—I sometimes imagine that the souls of the lost are compelled to walk through its streets perpetually. One feels them passing like a whif of air" (CL1 92). On 21 December 1888, Yeats linked his composition of "The Lake Isle of Innisfree" to his work on John Sherman: "In my story I make one of the charecters when ever he is in trouble long to go away and live alone on that Island—an old day dream of my own. Thinking over his feelings I made these verses about them . . ." (CL1 120–21). Then follows a draft of what many consider one of Yeats's finest early poems, the result of the interaction between life and art.

After *John Sherman*, Yeats would make one more attempt at realistic and autobiographical fiction. But though he worked on *The Speckled Bird* for several years, he failed to bring it to a satisfactory conclusion, and it was to remain unpublished during his lifetime. Yeats also began to register his dissatisfaction with *John Sherman and Dhoya*. As early as January 1895 he described it as "youthful" and "languid" (CL1 425). In October 1902, though, the work may well have been a topic of discussion during Yeats's first meeting with James Joyce.[21] In December of the same year he inscribed a copy to Lady Gregory (now in the Emory University Library) with a note of wistful regret:

> I don't think any of my Sligo relations—except possibly George Pollexfen—has ever read this Sligo story. One apologised to me every summer for not reading it, for several years. She used to say 'I had a copy once but somebody borrowed it[.]' I am sure that copy was given her. She would never have spent a 1/- on such a purpose.

In March 1904 he inscribed a copy of *John Sherman and*

Dhoya with the notation "all Sligo & Hammersmith."[22] Seven months later he inscribed another copy "Written when I was very young & knew no better."[23]

Thus, when Yeats began in 1907 to plan the contents and order of *The Collected Works in Verse and Prose*, it seems clear that he was hesitant to include *John Sherman and Dhoya*. However, by 12 July 1907 Yeats had agreed that one of the volumes would contain "The Secret Rose, John Sherman, Dhoya. (Very careful verbal revision necessary and two new stories desirable.)"[24] Eventually, *John Sherman and Dhoya*, with the subtitle *Two Early Stories*, appeared in volume seven of the *Collected Works*, published in December 1908; Yeats noted in a new preface that he had been "persuaded" to include them, "somewhat against my judgment."[25]

As copy for the new edition, Yeats asked the publisher to supply him with the 1891 text (L 491), which he then revised and submitted to the press on 14 November 1907, the date of the preface. A substantial portion of this material survives in the Shakespeare Birthplace Trust.[26] As these pages show only some of the changes in the printed version, Yeats must have made further revisions on the proofs. He was adamant that "I will not have one word printed that I have not seen and passed. . . . This will be my final text for many years, and I refuse to have any portion of that text settled by any person but myself" (L 485–86), and the version in the *Collected Works* is virtually devoid of error.

Although the revisions to *John Sherman and Dhoya* for the *Collected Works* do not significantly alter either story, they demonstrate that, as usual, Yeats did not neglect an opportunity to revise his work. In *John Sherman*, for instance, foreign words are eliminated: "*recherché*" becomes "distinguished" (I.i); the Gaelic "*gluggerabunthaun*" (I.1), meaning more or less "empty-rattling-arse," disappears. [27] The fictional "Inniscrewin" of 1891 is replaced by the real Innisfree (IV.1). [28] Other revisions produce a more restrained tone in the story. For instance, in 1891 "a clothes-moth in an antimacassar thought the end of the world had come and fluttered out"; in 1908 "a clothes-moth fluttered out" (II.ii). Likewise, "wildly" and "with a wild leap" are dropped from the account of Dhoya rushing to his death in the penultimate paragraph of the tale. Other changes are as minor as having a beetle crawl out of "its hole" rather than "his hole" (*John Sherman* I.ii).

After the appearance of the revised *John Sherman and Dhoya* in the 1908 *Collected Works*, Yeats for all intents and purposes exiled the stories from his canon. Although he was reminded of the work at least twice, inscribing copies of the first edition in 1920 and again ca. 1937–38, [29] there is no evidence that he gave any consideration to including *John Sherman and Dhoya* in *Early Poems and Stories* (1925) or in the Macmillan Edition de Luxe or the Scribner Dublin Edition of the 1930s. Nevertheless, having "read them for the first time these many years," he acknowledged in the 1908 preface that "They have come to interest me very deeply. . . ." If nothing else, Yeats's renewed "interest" is perhaps sufficient justification for the inclusion of *John Sherman and Dhoya* in the present Collected Edition of the Works.

NOTES

1. *The Collected Letters of W. B. Yeats: Volume One, 1865–1895*, ed. John Kelly (Oxford: Clarendon Press, 1986), p. 33. Hereafter cited as CL1.
2. *Memoirs*, ed. Denis Donoghue (New York: Macmillan, 1973),

p. 31. Yeats described this work as "a first rough draft of Memoirs made in 1916–17" (p. 19n1).

3. The Christmas issue probably contained a fairly long poem by Yeats, "How Ferencz Renyi Kept Silent," so to have included *Dhoya* as well would have been awkward. *The Gael* ceased publication shortly thereafter, possibly with the issue for 7 January 1888. See John S. Kelly, "Aesthete among the Athletes: Yeats's Contributions to *The Gael*," *Yeats* 2 (1984): 138.

4. *Uncollected Prose by W. B. Yeats, I: First Reviews and Articles, 1886–1896*, ed. John P. Frayne (New York: Columbia University Press, 1970), p. 104. Hereafter cited as UP1.

5. *Letters to the New Island*, ed. George Bornstein and Hugh Witemeyer (New York: Macmillan, 1989), p. 12. Hereafter cited as LNI. Cf. "There is no great literature without nationality, no great nationality without literature" (LNI 30).

6. W. G. Wood-Martin, *History of Sligo, County and Town* (Dublin: Hodges, Figgis, 1882–92), III: 221.

7. Reprinted from *The Gael* (27 April 1887) in "Aesthete among the Athletes," p. 91.

8. Either John Sherman was then rather different from the text that survives; or, more likely, Yeats was overstating his difficulty of avoiding symbolism in the narrative.

9. In another letter of the same month, the story is called "the Midnight Rider" (CL1 253). Yeats may have rejected the earlier titles when he recalled (or was reminded) that one of the tales in Lady Wilde's *Ancient Legends, Mystic Charms, and Superstitions of Ireland* (London: Ward and Downey, 1888) is called "The Midnight Ride."

10. Edward Dowden had briefly mentioned *John Sherman and Dhoya* while reviewing another work in the *Fortnightly Review* for November 1891. Father Russell's copy (a second edition, in paper) is preserved in the Beinecke Library at Yale University. Inscribing it, Yeats put quotation marks around "Ganconagh" and signed his name beneath. In order to be doubly sure that Father Russell would not forget the identity of the author of *John Sherman and Dhoya*, he also added the quotation marks and his signature on the front wrapper.

11. Reviewing a collected edition of William Allingham's poems in *United Ireland* ten days later, Yeats noted that his work "enshrined that passionate devotion that so many Irishmen feel for the little town where they were born, and for the mountains they saw from the doors they passed through in childhood. . . . He will always . . . be best loved by those who, like the present writer, have spent their childhood in some small Western seaboard town, and who remember how it was for years the centre of their world, and how its enclosing mountains and its quiet rivers became a portion of their life for ever" (UP1 210).

12. This copy, now at the Harry Ransom Humanities Research
    Center, University of Texas at Austin, is inscribed with the
    following poem:

    > We poets labour all our days
    > To make a little beauty be,
    > But vanquished by a woman's gaze
    > And the unlabouring stars are we:
    > So I—most lovely child of Eire—
    > Rising from labour, bow the knee
    > With equal reverence to the fire
    > Of the unlabouring stars and thee.

    The inscription is framed by a drawing by George W. Russell
    (AE). When Yeats copied the poem into a vellum manuscript
    book which he presented to Maud Gonne, called *The Flame of
    the Spirit*, he entitled it "Dedication of 'John Sherman and
    Dhoya.' " (For a transcription of that text as well as other man-
    uscript versions, see George Bornstein's forthcoming edition of
    The Early Poetry: Volume Two in the Cornell Yeats.)

    Earlier in the summer of 1891, Yeats may well have been
    hoping that *John Sherman and Dhoya* would be his engagement
    present to Maud; however, his proposal on 3 August 1891 was
    not accepted. Ironically, some years later Yeats's friend John
    Masefield would inscribe a copy of the first edition to his fiancée
    (collection of Richard J. Finneran).

13. The volume was published in New York as part of Cassell's
    " 'Unknown' Library." It was entered for copyright at the Li-
    brary of Congress on 2 October and received there on 10 No-
    vember 1891. There are some puzzling substantive differences
    between the 1891 London and New York editions. The most
    likely explanation is that the English text includes revisions
    which Yeats made on the proofs and which were not forwarded
    to America. *John Sherman and Dhoya*, ed. Richard J. Finneran
    (Detroit: Wayne State University Press, 1969), includes a col-
    lation of the variants between the 1891 and 1908 printings.

14. The anonymous review in *United Ireland* for 28 November 1891
    was of the "second edition," a fact which doubtless explains the
    comment that "the volume has already had a very considerable
    success" (p. 5). As noted above, the review copy sent to Father
    Russell was also a "second edition."

15. Allan Wade, *A Bibliography of the Writings of W. B. Yeats*, 3rd
    ed., rev. Russell K. Alspach (London: Rupert Hart-Davis, 1968),
    p. 24. The information presumably derives from A. J. A. Sy-
    mons, *A Bibliography of the First Editions of Books by William
    Butler Yeats* (London: The First Edition Club, 1924), p. 3.

16. The third edition is not in the British Library, the National Library of Ireland, or Yeats's own library. Copies can be found at the University of Washington and at Yale University. Its existence was not fully attested to until the 1958 second edition of Wade's *Bibliography*. In the 1951 first edition, Wade could only note that "a third edition was advertised in 1894" (p. 22). It is possible that Symons's citation of 2,000 copies includes this edition as well.

17. *W. B. Yeats, 1865–1939*, 2nd ed. (London: Macmillan, 1962), p. 77. The biography was first published in 1943.

    The note on Yeats's income in CL1 269n2 not only is based on an unlikely royalty of nearly 20 percent but also ignores the £10 from America as well as the lack of any royalty on the first 1,000 copies. Assuming that the second thousand of the first and second "editions" consisted of 178 hardcover and 822 paperback, Yeats would have earned slightly less than £8 with a 10 percent royalty or slightly less than £10 with a 12.5 percent royalty. In short, he probably earned ca. £18–20 from the British and American 1891 editions combined. For Hone's £40 to be correct, then, Yeats would have had to have earned another £20 on the third edition, which is extremely improbable.

18. The review has been identified as "probably by John F. Taylor" (CL1 272n3). If so, Yeats was initially unaware of that fact, asking O'Leary on ca. 4 December 1891, "Have you heard what Taylor thought of Sherman? (CL1 276). However, on 23 August 1892 he told Unwin "If you would send a copy of 'the Countess Kathleen' to J F Taylor . . . he will review it in the Manchester Guardian" (CL1 309), which may indicate that by then he knew. Yeats and Taylor, however, were shortly to quarrel over the New Irish Library, and *The Countess Kathleen* was not reviewed in the *Manchester Guardian*.

19. "William Butler Yeats's *John Sherman*: An Irish Poet's Declaration of Independence," *Irish University Review* 9:1 (Spring 1979): 93.

20. *Autobiographies* (London: Macmillan, 1955), p. 49. See p. 27 for the remark about Sligo versus London. Murphy (p. 101) has identified Agnes Pollexfen as the speaker.

21. Joyce's copy of *John Sherman and Dhoya* is inscribed "Jas A Joyce. Dublin 1902." See the sale catalogue, *Modern Literature from the Library of James Gilvarry*, Christie's (New York), 7 February 1986, item #393, p. 149; present whereabouts of this copy unknown.

    The fullest account of the meeting is in Richard Ellmann, *James Joyce*, rev. ed. (Oxford and New York: Oxford University Press, 1982), pp. 100–104. Yeats's unpublished account of the occasion, at first intended as a Preface for *Ideas of Good and Evil*

(1903), recapitulates the contrast developed in *John Sherman* between the town, especially "big towns like London," and the country, especially "in Ireland and in places where the towns have not been able to call the tune" (p. 103).

Without, I think, knowing that Joyce owned a copy of *John Sherman and Dhoya*, Brendan O Hehir once commented that "I could not but wonder if the young Joyce's naughty alleged remark that Yeats was too old to be helped by him was not, if true, stimulated by Yeats's stories. Certainly the author of *Dubliners* was more advanced in technique than the author of *John Sherman*, whereas the author of *Chamber Music* could have nothing valuable to say to the poet Yeats" (letter to Richard J. Finneran, 16 January 1970).

22. *Modern Literature from the Library of James Gilvarry*, item 468, p. 181; present whereabouts unknown.

23. Quoted in Wade, *Bibliography*, p. 24. The inscription was in Paul Lemperly's copy; present whereabouts unknown.

24. *The Letters of W. B. Yeats*, ed. Allan Wade (London: Rupert Hart-Davis, 1954), p. 488. Hereafter cited as L. The full text of Yeats's letter of 8 July 1907 to Bullen—of which Wade prints only a fragment (L 486–87)—makes it clear that "two new stories desirable" refers to potential replacements not for *John Sherman and Dhoya* but for two of the tales in *The Secret Rose* (National Library of Ireland MS. 30,568).

25. In a diary used as a notebook, preserved in the Shakespeare Birthplace Trust (ER 136/74), A. H. Bullen (the publisher of the 1908 *Collected Works*) either composed or copied a favorable commentary on *John Sherman*: "not merely a clever story of the artistic temperament," "something more subtle, more elusive, and of more lasting value" (entry for 24–26 June). It thus seems likely that the "persuasion" was his. Yeats, on the other hand, was insistent about the subtitle "Two Early Stories," telling Bullen in an undated letter that *John Sherman and Dhoya* "comes last in the book & are to be labelled early work—that is essential" (University of Kansas Library).

26. Catalogued as ER 136/63, the unbound pages lack pp. 47–48, 77–112, 131–42, and all of *Dhoya* (pp. 171–95). Conrad A. Balliet's *W. B. Yeats: A Census of the Manuscripts* (New York & London: Garland Publishing, 1990) incorrectly states that the archive includes "revised proofs" (p. 26).

27. Brendan O Hehir has provided the following analysis of *gluggerabunthaun*: "To say what it literally means requires first its analysis into Irish words, and analysis unfortunately produces two disjunct possibilities. It is either *glagar a' buntáin* or *glagaire-buntán*. *Glagar* means primarily 'rattle'—the sound of rattling, a rattling sound. By figurative extension it means 'boasting,'

'prating.' *Glagaire* is anything that rattles—a toy rattle, an addled egg, a pod or husk containing loose seeds—and by figurative extension 'boaster, prater.' *Bun* means 'bottom' in a generally neutral sense, but it can mean 'fundament' or 'anus.' *Bundún* means, among other things, a prolapsed anus or the prolapsed fundament of a fowl consequent upon egg-laying. *Buntán* can very readily appear as a dialect variation of *bundún*. The suffix -[*t*]*an*, however, often indicates, in a somewhat derogatory sense, a thing or person characterized by the attribute suggested by the word to which it is attached. *Buntán* therefore could mean a thing or person having a *bun*, it could also overlay *bundún*, so that possibly in some dialect a *buntán* might be say a goose with a prolapsed fundament. The first phrase above therefore might be interpreted as 'rattle of a prolapsed anus' or 'rattle of a person-with-a-prolapsed-anus'—'rattle' possibly meaning 'boasting' in either case. The second phrase might be interpreted as 'person-with-a-rattling-arse' or 'rattle-arse' or 'rattle-prolapsed fundament' or 'rattle-prolapsed-fundament-ist.' Throughout the notion of farting is perhaps not absent. If forced to a single interpretation I would say: An approximate translation would be 'empty-rattling-arse' " (letter to Richard J. Finneran, 18 January 1968).

In his seminal "Yeats and the Irish Language," *Yeats* 1 (1983): 92–103, O Hehir has further commented that "When Yeats used the word he probably had no idea of its meaning anything much more derogatory than 'Jack o'Dreams'—perhaps as a Gaelic synonym. But before 1908 he had got wind—if I may so put it— of the term's true sense, and found it too crude an epithet to apply to his own surrogate: another instance of Gaelic harshness beneath the mellifluous syllables" (p. 97).

28. Brendan O Hehir has offered the following analysis of "Inniscrewin": "As it stands it looks dubious to me. '*Innis*'—that is to say *Inis*—means 'island.' Innisfree is *Inis Fraoigh*, 'Heather Island,' but if Inniscrewin is a real name some word has been distorted beyond recognition into 'crewin.' *Cruan* is an adjective meaning red or orange; *cruinn* (pronounced krin, however) an adjective meaning circular or complete. There is a Loughcrew in Meath: *Loch Craoibhe*, where *craoibhe* means 'branchy,' but I see no way to get that -in on the end. Cruninish is an island in Lough Erne in Co. Fermanagh (about 40 miles east of Sligo town) and is possibly *crón inis* (copperbrown island)" (letter to Richard J. Finneran, 18 January 1968). Further, " 'Inniscrewin' could be 'Crewinish' turned around, but with the median -in syllable repeated. This would make sense if Yeats was somehow aware that 'Crewinish' meant 'branchy island'—an apt substitution for 'Innisfree,' . . . but unfortunately garbled in the trans-

position. So I adopt two contrary hypotheses—1) Yeats reached for an Irish-sounding name, with no sense or the dimmest sense of its possible meaning; 2) with somebody's aid he concocted an ingenious (but erroneous) disguise for Sligo" (letter to Richard J. Finneran, 27 January 1968).

Eamonn de hOir of the Ordnance Survey Office, Dublin, has offered an alternative commentary on "Inniscrewin": "In form Inniscrewin immediately suggests the town of Inishcrone in the west of co. Sligo on the shore of Killala Bay. Although some distance from Sligo town, this was and is a well-known holiday resort and would certainly have been known to Yeats, at least by name. The name derives from Irish *inis eiscir* (or, *eiscreash*) *abhann*, 'the inis of the esker (= sand or gravel ridge) of the river.' There is now no island here and it seems more probable that inis in this case means a 'milking-place' or a 'river meadow.' . . . [O]ne late 16th century form we have noted of the name, Inyschrewin, . . . is very like the form used by Yeats. Although it does not seem that inis means 'island' in the case of Inishcrone, that would be the first meaning to spring to mind and Yeats may well have thought it meant 'island' here as in many other cases of which he would be aware" (letter to Richard J. Finneran, 31 January 1968).

Even though Yeats admitted in the new preface that "Sligo . . . is Ballah," he continued to use "Ballah" in the 1908 text. In part, "Ballah" is a more typical Irish placename than Sligo. As O Hehir has noted, two of the towns near Sligo are called Balla and Ballina, and "Ballagh, Ballah, and Bally, meaning respectively 'way,' 'fordmouth,' and 'town,' are frequent elements in the names of Irish towns and villages" (letter to Richard J. Finneran, 27 January 1968). In addition, "Ballah" may have been retained because of its echoes of Blake's "Beulah," described by Yeats and Edwin John Ellis in *The Works of William Blake* (London: Bernard Quaritch, 1893) as "a place of repose, ante-chamber of Inspiration, and dwelling of the muses" (I: 260).

29. See Balliet, *Census*, p. 26.

A NOTE ON THE TEXT

The copy-text for this edition is *John Sherman and Dhoya: Two Early Stories* in volume seven of *The Collected Works in Verse & Prose*, published in December 1908 by the Shakespeare Head Press in Stratford-on-Avon. As Yeats carefully read proofs for that edition, only five emendations have been required, all to *John Sherman*. In I.ii (seventeenth paragraph, first sentence), a comma has been added after "Sherman," as in the 1891 American edition. In I.iii (ninth paragraph, second sentence), "longed" has been emended to "longer," as in the 1891–92 printings. In III.iii (fifteenth paragraph, first sentence), a double quotation mark has been corrected to a single quotation mark. In IV.iii (second paragraph, penultimate sentence), "illusion" has been emended to "allusion," as in the 1891–92 printings. In V.ii (third paragraph, first sentence), "beside" has been emended to "besides," as in the 1891 American edition.

In the present edition, all compound words hyphenated at line-end are to be considered hyphenated forms. Ambiguous line-end hyphenation in the copy-text has been adjudicated based on the occurrence of the word elsewhere in the 1908 and/or 1891 editions. In three instances where such evidence was inconclusive, the hyphenated form of the copy-text has been retained: "vine-trees" ([Preface], last sentence); "house-maid" (*John Sherman* II.ii, second paragraph, last sentence); "quicken-berry" (*Dhoya* III, penultimate paragraph, eleventh sentence).

The text of "Ganconagh's Apology," which was not reprinted in the *Collected Works*, has been taken from the first 1891 English edition. No emendations have been required.

Superscript numbers in the text refer to the editor's explanatory notes.

John Sherman

AND

Dhoya

[PREFACE]

Having been persuaded somewhat against my judgment to include these early stories, I have read them for the first time these many years. They have come to interest me very deeply; for I am something of an astrologer, and can see in them a young man—was I twenty-three? and we Irish ripen slowly[1]—born when the Water-Carrier was on the horizon, at pains to overcome Saturn in Saturn's hour, just as I can see in much that follows his struggle with the still all-too-unconquered Moon, and at last, as I think, the summons of the prouder Sun.[2] Sligo, where I had lived as a child and spent some months or weeks of every year till long after, is Ballah, and Pool Dhoya is at the river mouth there,[3] and he who gave me all of Sherman that was not born at the rising of the Water-Carrier has still the bronze upon his face, and is at this moment, it may be, in his walled garden, wondering, as he did twenty years ago, whether he will ever mend the broken glass of the conservatory, where I am not too young to recollect the vine-trees and grapes that did not ripen.[4]

W. B. YEATS.

November 14th, 1907.

JOHN SHERMAN

FIRST PART

JOHN SHERMAN LEAVES BALLAH

I

In the west of Ireland, on the 9th of December, in the town of Ballah, in the Imperial Hotel¹ there was a single guest, clerical and youthful. With the exception of a stray commercial traveller, who stopped once for a night, there had been nobody for a whole month but this guest, and now he was thinking of going away. The town, full enough in summer of trout and salmon fishers, slept all winter like the bears.

On the evening of the 9th of December, in the coffee-room of the Imperial Hotel, there was nobody but this guest. The guest was irritated. It had rained all day, and now that it was clearing up night had almost fallen. He had packed his portmanteau; his stockings, his clothes-brush, his razor, his dress shoes were each in their corner, and now he had nothing to do. He had tried the paper that was lying on the table. He did not agree with its politics.

The waiter was playing an accordion in a little room over the stairs. The guest's irritation increased, for the more he thought about it the more he perceived that the accordion was badly played. There was a piano in the coffee-room; he sat down at it and played the tune correctly, as loudly as possible. The waiter took no notice. He did not know that he was being played for. He was wholly absorbed in his own playing, and besides he was old, obstinate, and deaf. The guest could stand it no longer. He rang for the waiter, and then, remembering that he did not need anything, went out before he came. He went through Martin's Street and Peter's Lane, and turned down by the burnt house at the corner of the fish-market, picking his way towards the bridge. The town was dripping, but the rain was almost over. The large drops fell seldomer and seldomer into the puddles. It was the hour of ducks. Three or four had squeezed themselves under a gate, and were now splashing about in the gutter of the main street. There was scarcely anyone abroad. Once or twice a countryman went by in yellow gaiters covered with mud and looked at the guest. Once an old woman with a basket of clothes, recognizing the Protestant curate's *locum tenens*,[2] made a low curtsey.

The clouds gradually drifted away, the twilight deepened and the stars came out. The guest, having bought some cigarettes, had spread his waterproof on the parapet of the bridge and was now leaning his elbows upon it, looking at the river and feeling at last quite tranquil. His meditations, he repeated, to himself, were plated with silver by the stars. The water slid noiselessly, and one or two of the larger stars made little roadways of fire into the darkness. The light from a distant casement made also its roadway. Once or twice a fish leaped. Along the banks were the vague shadows of houses, seeming like phantoms gathering to drink.

Yes; he felt now quite contented with the world. Amidst his enjoyment of the shadows and the river—a veritable festival of silence—was mixed pleasantly the knowledge that, as he leant there with the light of a neighbouring gas-jet flickering faintly on his refined form and nervous face and glancing from the little medal of some Anglican order that hung upon his watch-guard, he must have seemed—if there had been any to witness—a being of a different kind to the inhabitants —at once rough and conventional—of this half-deserted town. Between these two feelings the unworldly and the worldly tossed a leaping wave of perfect enjoyment. How pleasantly conscious of his own identity it made him when he thought how he and not those whose birthright it was, felt most the beauty of these shadows and this river! For him who had read much, seen operas and plays, known religious experiences, and written verse to a waterfall in Switzerland, and not for those who dwelt upon its borders for their whole lives, did this river raise a tumult of images and wonders. What meaning it had for them he could not imagine. Some meaning surely it must have!

As he gazed out into the darkness, spinning a web of thoughts from himself to the river, from the river to himself, he saw, with a corner of his eye, a spot of red light moving in the air at the other end of the bridge. He turned towards it. It came closer and closer, there appearing behind it the while a man and a cigar. The man carried in one hand a mass of fishing-line covered with hooks, and in the other a tin porringer full of bait.

'Good evening, Howard.'

'Good evening,' answered the guest, taking his el-bows off the parapet and looking in a preoccupied way at the man with the hooks. It was only gradually he remembered that he was in Ballah among the barbarians, for his mind had strayed from the last evening flies, making circles on the water beneath, to the devil's song against 'the little spirits' in *Mefistofele*.[3] Looking down at the stone parapet he considered a moment and then burst out—

'Sherman, how do you stand this place—you who have thoughts above mere eating and sleeping and are not always grinding at the stubble mill? Here everybody lives in the eighteenth century—the squalid century. Well, I am going to-morrow, you know. Thank Heaven, I am done with your grey streets and grey minds! The curate must come home, sick or well. I have a religious essay to write, and besides I should die. Think of that old fellow at the corner there, our most important parishioner. There are no more hairs on his head than thoughts in his skull. To merely look at him is to rob life of its dignity. Then there is nothing in the shops but school-books and Sunday-school prizes. Excellent, no doubt, for anyone who has not had to read as many as I have. Such a choir! such rain!'

'You need some occupation peculiar to the place,' said the other, baiting his hooks with worms out of the little porringer. 'I catch eels. You should set some night-lines too. You bait them with worms in this way, and put them among the weeds at the edge of the river. In the morning you find an eel or two, if you have good fortune, turning round and round and making the weeds sway. I shall catch a great many after this rain.'

'What a suggestion! Do you mean to stay here,' said Howard, 'till your mind rots like our most important parishioner's?'

'No, no! To be quite frank with you,' replied the other, 'I have some good looks and shall try to turn them to account by going away from here pretty soon and trying to persuade some girl with money to fall in love with me. I shall not be altogether a bad match, you see, because after she has made me a little prosperous

my uncle will die and make me much more so. I wish
to be able always to remain a lounger. Yes, I shall marry
money. My mother has set her heart on it, and I am
not, you see, the kind of person who falls in love
inconveniently. For the present—'

'You are vegetating,' interrupted the other.

'No, I am seeing the world. In your big towns a man
finds his minority and knows nothing outside its border.
He knows only the people like himself. But here one
chats with the whole world in a day's walk, for every
man one meets is a class. The knowledge I am picking
up may be useful to me when I enter the great cities and
their ignorance. But I have lines to set. Come with me.
I would ask you home, but you and my mother, you
know, do not get on well.'

'I could not live with anyone I did not believe in,'
said Howard; 'you are so different from me. You can
live with mere facts, and that is why, I suppose, your
schemes are so mercenary. Before this beautiful river,
these stars, these great purple shadows, do you not feel
like an insect in a flower? As for me, I also have planned
my future. Not too near or too far from a great city, I
see myself in a cottage with diamond panes, sitting by
the fire. There are books everywhere and etchings on
the wall; on the table is a manuscript essay on some
religious matter. Perhaps I shall marry some day. Probably not, for I shall ask so much. Certainly I shall not
marry for money, for I hold that when we have lost the
directness and sincerity of our nature we have no com-
pass. If we once break it the world grows trackless.'

'Good-bye,' said Sherman, briskly; 'I have baited the
last hook. Your schemes suit you, but a sluggish fellow
like me, poor devil, who wishes to lounge through the
world, would find them expensive.'

They parted; Sherman to set his lines and Howard
to his hotel in high spirits, for it seemed to him he had
been eloquent. The billiard-room, which opened on the
street, was lighted up. A few young men came round
to play sometimes. He went in, for among these pro-
vincial youths he felt distinguished; besides, he was a
really good player. As he came in one of the players
missed and swore. Howard reproved him with a look.
He joined the play for a time, and then catching sight
through a distant door of the hotel-keeper's wife putting
a kettle on the hob he hurried off, and, drawing a chair
to the fire, began one of those long gossips about
everybody's affairs peculiar to the cloth.

As Sherman, having set his lines, returned home, he
passed a tobacconist's—a sweet-shop and tobacconist's
in one—the only shop in town, except public-houses,
that remained open. The tobacconist was standing in his
door, and, recognizing one who dealt consistently with
a rival at the other end of the town, muttered: 'There
goes that Jack o' Dreams; been fishing most likely. Ugh!'
Sherman paused for a moment as he repassed the bridge
and looked at the water, on which now a new-risen and
crescent moon was shining dimly. How full of memories it was to him! what playmates and boyish adven-
tures did it not bring to mind! To him it seemed to say,
'Stay near to me,' as to Howard it had said, 'Go yonder,
to those other joys and other sceneries I have told you
of.' It bade him who loved stay still and dream, and
gave flying feet to him who imagined.

II

The house where Sherman and his mother lived was
one of those bare houses so common in country towns.

Their dashed fronts mounting above empty pavements have a kind of dignity in their utilitarianism. They seem to say, 'Fashion has not made us, nor ever do its caprices pass our sand-cleaned doorsteps.' On every basement window is the same dingy wire blind; on every door the same brass knocker. Custom everywhere! 'So much the longer,' the blinds seem to say, 'have eyes glanced through us'; and the knockers to murmur, 'And fingers lifted us.'

No. 15, Stephens' Row, was in no manner peculiar among its twenty fellows. The chairs in the drawing-room facing the street were of heavy mahogany with horsehair cushions worn at the corners. On the round table was somebody's commentary on the New Testament laid like the spokes of a wheel on a table-cover of American oilcloth with stamped Japanese figures half worn away. The room was seldom used, for Mrs. Sherman was solitary because silent. In this room the dressmaker sat twice a year, and here the rector's wife used every month or so to drink a cup of tea. It was quite clean. There was not a fly-mark on the mirror, and all summer the fern in the grate was constantly changed. Behind this room and overlooking the garden was the parlour, where cane-bottomed chairs took the place of mahogany. Sherman had lived here with his mother all his life, and their old servant hardly remembered having lived anywhere else; and soon she would absolutely cease to remember the world she knew before she saw the four walls of this house, for every day she forgot something fresh. The son was almost thirty, the mother fifty, and the servant near seventy. Every year they had two hundred pounds among them, and once a year the son got a new suit of clothes and went into the drawing-room to look at himself in the mirror.

On the morning of the 10th of December Mrs. Sherman was down before her son. A spare, delicate-featured woman, with somewhat thin lips tightly closed as with silent people, and eyes at once gentle and distrustful, tempering the hardness of the lips. She helped the servant to set the table, and then, for her old-fashioned ideas would not allow her to rest, began to knit, often interrupting her knitting to go into the kitchen or to listen at the foot of the stairs. At last, hearing a sound upstairs, she put the eggs down to boil, muttering the while, and began again to knit. When her son appeared she received him with a smile.

'Late again, mother,' he said.

'The young should sleep,' she answered, for to her he seemed still a boy.

She had finished her breakfast some time before the young man, and because it would have appeared very wrong to her to leave the table, she sat on knitting behind the tea-urn: an industry the benefit of which was felt by many poor children—almost the only neighbours she had a good word for.

'Mother,' said the young man, presently, 'your friend the *locum tenens* is off to-day.'

'A good riddance.'

'Why are you so hard on him? He talked intelligently when here, I thought,' answered her son.

'I do not like his theology,' she replied, 'nor his way of running about and flirting with this body and that body, nor his way of chattering while he buttons and unbuttons his gloves.'

'You forget he is a man of the great world, and has about him a manner that must seem strange to us.'

'Oh, he might do very well,' she answered, 'for one of those Carton girls at the rectory.'

'That eldest girl is a good girl,' replied her son.

'She looks down on us all, and thinks herself intel-
lectual,' she went on. 'I remember when girls were content with their catechism and their Bibles and a little
practice at the piano, maybe, for an accomplishment.
What does any one want more? It is all pride.'

'You used to like her as a child,' said the young man.

'I like all children.'

Sherman, having finished his breakfast, took a book
of travels in one hand and a trowel in the other and went
out into the garden. Having looked under the parlour
window for the first tulip shoots, he went down to the
further end and began covering some sea-kale for forcing. He had not been long at work when the servant
brought him a letter. There was a stone roller at one
side of the grass plot. He sat down upon it, and taking
the letter between his finger and thumb began looking
at it with an air that said: 'Well! I know what you mean.'
He remained long thus without opening it, the book
lying beside him on the roller.

The garden—the letter—the book! You have there
the three symbols of his life. Every morning he worked
in that garden among the sights and sounds of nature.
Month by month he planted and hoed and dug there.
In the middle he had set a hedge that divided the garden
in two. Above the hedge were flowers; below it, vegetables. At the furthest end from the house, lapping
broken masonry full of wallflowers, the river said,
month after month to all upon its banks, 'Hush!' He
dined at two with perfect regularity, and in the afternoon
went out to shoot or walk. At twilight he set night-
lines. Later on he read. He had not many books—a
Shakespeare, Mungo Park's travels, a few two-shilling
novels, *Percy's Reliques*, and a volume on etiquette.[4] He

seldom varied his occupations. He had no profession. The town talked of it. They said: 'He lives upon his mother,' and were very angry. They never let him see this, however, for it was generally understood he would be a dangerous fellow to rouse; but there was an uncle from whom Sherman had expectations who sometimes wrote remonstrating. Mrs. Sherman resented these letters, for she was afraid of her son going away to seek his fortune—perhaps even in America. Now this matter preyed somewhat on Sherman. For three years or so he had been trying to make his mind up and come to some decision. Sometimes when reading he would start and press his lips together and knit his brows for a moment.

It will now be seen why the garden, the book, and the letter were the three symbols of his life, summing up as they did his love of out-of-door doings, his meditations, his anxieties. His life in the garden had granted serenity to his forehead, the reading of his few books had filled his eyes with reverie, and the feeling that he was not quite a good citizen had given a slight and occasional trembling to his lips.

He opened the letter. Its contents were what he had long expected. His uncle offered to take him into his office. He laid it spread out before him—a foot on each margin, right and left—and looked at it, turning the matter over and over in his mind. Would he go? would he stay? He did not like the idea much. The lounger in him did not enjoy the thought of London. Gradually his mind wandered away into scheming—infinite scheming—what would he do if he went, what would he do if he did not go?

A beetle, attracted by the faint sunlight, had crawled out of its hole. It saw the paper and crept on to it, the better to catch the sunlight. Sherman saw the beetle but his mind was not occupied with it. 'Shall I tell Mary Carton?' he was thinking. Mary had long been his adviser and friend. She was, indeed, everybody's adviser. Yes, he would ask her what to do. Then again he thought—no, he would decide for himself. The beetle began to move. 'If it goes off the paper by the top I will ask her—if by the bottom I will not.'

The beetle went off by the top. He got up with an air of decision and went into the tool-house and began sorting seeds and picking out the light ones, sometimes stopping to watch a spider; for he knew he must wait till the afternoon to see Mary Carton. The tool-house was a favourite place with him. He often read there and watched the spiders in the corners.

At dinner he was preoccupied.

'Mother,' he said, 'would you much mind if we went away from this?'

'I have often told you,' she answered, 'I do not like one place better than another. I like them all equally little.'

After dinner he went again into the tool-house. This time he did not sort seeds—only watched the spiders.

III

Towards evening he went out. The pale sunshine of winter flickered on his path. The wind blew the straws about. He grew more and more melancholy. A dog of his acquaintance was chasing rabbits in a field. He had never been known to catch one, and since his youth had never seen one, for he was almost wholly blind. They were his form of the eternal chimera. The dog left the field and followed with a friendly sniff.

They came together to the rectory. Mary Carton was not in. There was a children's practice in the school-house. They went thither.

A child of four or five with a swelling on its face was sitting under a wall opposite the school door, waiting to make faces at the Protestant children as they came out. Catching sight of the dog she seemed to debate in her mind whether to throw a stone at it or call it to her. She threw the stone and made it run. In after times he remembered all these things as though they were of importance.

He opened the latched green door and went in. About twenty children were singing in shrill voices, standing in a row at the further end. At the harmonium he recognised Mary Carton, who nodded to him and went on with her playing. The whitewashed walls were covered with glazed prints of animals; at the further end was a large map of Europe; by a fire at the near end was a table with the remains of tea. This tea was an idea of Mary's. They had tea and cake first, afterwards the singing. The floor was covered with crumbs. The fire was burning brightly. Sherman sat down beside it. A child with a great deal of oil in her hair was sitting on the end of a form at the other side.

'Look,' she whispered, 'I have been sent away. At any rate they are further from the fire. They have to be near the harmonium. I would not sing. Do you like hymns? I don't. Will you have a cup of tea? I can make it quite well. See, I did not spill a drop. Have you enough milk?' It was a cup full of milk—children's tea. 'Look, there is a mouse carrying away a crumb. Hush!'

They sat there, the child watching the mouse, Sherman pondering on his letter, until the music ceased and the children came tramping down the room. The mouse having fled, Sherman's self-appointed hostess got up with a sigh and went out with the others.

Mary Carton closed the harmonium and came towards Sherman. Her face and all her movements showed a gentle decision of character. Her glance was serene, her features regular, her figure at the same time ample and beautifully moulded; her dress plain yet not without a certain air of distinction. In a different society she would have had many suitors. But she was of a type that in country towns does not get married at all. Its beauty is too lacking in pink and white, its nature in that small assertiveness admired for character by the uninstructed. Elsewhere she would have known her own beauty—as it is right that all the beautiful should —and have learnt how to display it, to add gesture to her calm and more of mirth and smiles to her grave cheerfulness. As it was, her manner was much older than herself.

She sat down by Sherman with the air of an old friend. They had long been accustomed to consult together on every matter. They were such good friends they had never fallen in love with each other. Perfect love and perfect friendship are indeed incompatible; for the one is a battlefield where shadows war beside the combatants, and the other a placid country where Consultation has her dwelling.

These two were such good friends that the most gossiping townspeople had given them up with a sigh. The doctor's wife, a faded beauty and devoted romance reader, said one day, as they passed, 'They are such cold creatures'; the old maid who kept the Berlin-wool[5] shop remarked, 'They are not of the marrying sort'; and now their comings and goings were no longer noticed. Nothing had ever come to break in on their quiet companionship and give obscurity as a dwelling-place for the needed illusions. Had one been weak and the other strong, one plain and the other handsome, one guide and the other guided, one wise and the other foolish, love might have found them out in a moment, for love is based on inequality as friendship is on equality.

'John,' said Mary Carton, warming her hands at the fire, 'I have had a troublesome day. Did you come to help me teach the children to sing? It was good of you: you were just too late.'

'No,' he answered, 'I have come to be your pupil. I am always your pupil.'

'Yes, and a most disobedient one.'

'Well, advise me this time at any rate. My uncle has written, offering me a hundred pounds a year to begin with in his London office. Am I to go?'

'You know quite well my answer,' she said.

'Indeed I do not. Why should I go? I am contented here. I am now making my garden ready for spring. Later on there will be trout fishing and saunters by the edge of the river in the evening when the bats are flickering about. In July there will be races. I enjoy the bustle. I enjoy life here. When anything annoys me I keep away from it, that is all. You know I am always busy. I have occupation and friends and am quite contented.'

'It is a great loss to many of us, but you must go, John,' she said. 'For you know you will be old some day, and perhaps when the vitality of youth is gone you will feel that your life is empty and find that you are too old to change it; and you will give up, perhaps, trying to be happy and likeable and become as the rest are. I think I can see you,' she said, with a laugh, 'a hypochondriac, like Gorman, the retired excise officer, or with a red nose like Dr. Stephens, or growing like Peters, the elderly cattle merchant, who starves his horse.'

'They were bad material to begin with,' he answered, 'and, besides, I cannot take my mother away with me at her age, and I cannot leave her alone.'

'What annoyance it may be,' she answered, 'will soon be forgotten. You will be able to give her many more comforts. We women—we all like to be dressed well and have pleasant rooms to sit in, and a young man at your age should not be idle. You must go away from this little backward place. We shall miss you, but you are clever and must go and work with other men and have your talents admitted.'

'How emulous you would have me! Perhaps I shall be well-to-do some day; meanwhile I only wish to stay here with my friends.'

She went over to the window and looked out with her face turned from him. The evening light cast a long shadow behind her on the floor. After some moments, she said, 'I see people ploughing on the slope of the hill. There are people working on a house to the right. Everywhere there are people busy,' and with a slight tremble in her voice she added, 'and, John, nowhere are there any doing what they wish. One has to think of so many things—of duty and God.'

'Mary, I didn't know you were so religious.'

Coming towards him with a smile, she said, 'No more did I, perhaps. But sometimes the self in one is very strong. One has to think a great deal and reason with it. Yet I try hard to lose myself in things about me. These children now—I often lie awake thinking about them. That child who was talking to you is often on my mind. I do not know what will happen to her. She makes me unhappy. I am afraid she is not a good child at all. I am afraid she is not taught well at home. I try hard to be gentle and patient with her. I am a little displeased with myself to-day, so I have lectured you. There! I have made my confession. But,' she added, taking one of his hands in both hers and reddening, 'you must go away. You must not be idle. You will gain everything.'

As she stood there with bright eyes, the light of evening about her, Sherman for perhaps the first time saw how beautiful she was, and was flattered by her interest. For the first time also her presence did not make him at peace with the world.

'Will you be an obedient pupil?'

'You know so much more than I do,' he answered, 'and are so much wiser. I will write to my uncle and agree to his offer.'

'Now you must go home,' she said. 'You must not keep your mother waiting for her tea. There! I have raked the fire out. We must not forget to lock the door behind us.'

As they stood on the doorstep the wind blew a whirl of dead leaves about them.

'They are my old thoughts,' he said; 'see, they are all withered.'

They walked together silently. At the vicarage he left her and went homeward.

The deserted flour-store at the corner of two roads,

the house that had been burnt hollow ten years before and still lifted its blackened beams, the straggling and leafless fruit-trees rising above garden walls, the church where he was christened—these foster-mothers of his infancy seemed to nod and shake their heads over him.

'Mother,' he said, hurriedly entering the room, 'we are going to London.'

'As you wish. I always knew you would be a rolling stone,' she answered, and went out to tell the servant that as soon as she had finished the week's washing they must pack up everything, for they were going to London.

'Yes, we must pack up,' said the old peasant; she did not stop peeling the onion in her hand—she had not comprehended. In the middle of the night she suddenly started up in bed with a pale face and a prayer to the Virgin[6] whose image hung over her head—she had now comprehended.

IV

On January the 5th, about two in the afternoon, Sherman sat on the deck of the steamer *Lavinia*[7] enjoying a period of sunshine between two showers. The steamer *Lavinia* was a cattle-boat. It had been his wish to travel by some more expensive route, but his mother, with her old-fashioned ideas of duty, would not hear of it, and now, as he foresaw, was extremely uncomfortable below, while he, who was a good sailor, was pretty happy on deck, and would have been quite so if the pigs would only tire of their continual squealing. With the exception of a very dirty old woman sitting by a crate of geese, all the passengers but himself were below. This old woman made the journey monthly with geese for the Liverpool market.

Sherman was dreaming. He began to feel very desolate, and commenced a letter to Mary Carton in his notebook to state this fact. He was a laborious and unpractised writer, and found it helped him to make a pencil copy. Sometimes he stopped and watched the puffins sleeping on the waves. Each one of them had its head tucked in in a somewhat different way. 'That is because their characters are different,' he thought.

Gradually he began to notice a great many corks floating by, one after the other. The old woman saw them too, and said, waking out of a half sleep: 'Misther John Sherman, we will be in the Mersey[8] before evening. Why are ye goin' among them savages in London, Misther John? Why don't ye stay among your own people—for what have we in this life but a mouthful of air?'

SECOND PART

MARGARET LELAND

I

Sherman and his mother rented a small house on the north side of St. Peter's Square, Hammersmith.[9] The front windows looked out on to the old rank and green square, the windows behind on to a little patch of garden round which the houses gathered and pressed as though they already longed to trample it out. In this garden was a single tall pear tree that never bore fruit.

Three years passed by without any notable event. Sherman went every day to his office in Tower Hill Street, abused his work a great deal, and was not unhappy perhaps. He was probably a bad clerk, but then nobody was very exacting with the nephew of the head of the firm.

The firm of Sherman and Saunders, ship-brokers, was a long-established, old-fashioned house. Saunders had been dead some years and old Michael Sherman ruled alone—an old bachelor full of family pride and pride in his wealth. He lived, for all that, in a very simple fashion. His mahogany furniture was a little solider than other people's perhaps. He did not understand display. Display finds its excuse in some taste good or bad, and in a long industrious life Michael Sherman had never found leisure to form one. He seemed to live only from habit. Year by year he grew more silent, gradually ceasing to regard anything but his family and his ships. His family were represented by his nephew and his nephew's mother. He did not feel much affection for them. He believed in his family—that was all. To remind him of the other goal of his thoughts hung round his private office pictures with such inscriptions as 'S.S. *Indus* at the Cape of Good Hope,' 'The barque *Mary* in the Mozambique Channel,' 'The barque *Livingstone* at Port Said,'[10] and many more. Every rope was drawn accurately with a ruler, and here and there were added distant vessels sailing proudly by with all that indifference to perspective peculiar to the drawings of sailors. On every ship was the flag of the firm spread out to show the letters.

No man cared for old Michael Sherman. Every one liked John. Both were silent, but the young man had sometimes a talkative fit. The old man lived for his ledger, the young man for his dreams.

In spite of all these differences, the uncle was on the whole pleased with the nephew. He noticed a certain stolidity that was of the family. It sometimes irritated others. It pleased him. He saw a hundred indications besides that made him say, 'He is a true Sherman. We Shermans begin that way and give up frivolity as we grow old. We are all the same in the end.'

Mrs. Sherman and her son had but a small round of acquaintances—a few rich people, clients of the house of Sherman and Saunders for the most part. Among these was a Miss Margaret Leland who lived with her mother, the widow of the late Henry Leland, shipbroker, on the eastern side of St. Peter's Square. Their house was larger than the Shermans', and noticeable among its fellows by the newly-painted hall-door. Within on every side were bronzes and china vases and heavy curtains. In all were displayed the curious and vagrant taste of Margaret Leland: the rich Italian and mediæval draperies of pre-Raphaelite[11] taste jostling the brightest and vulgarest products of more native and Saxon schools; vases of the most artistic shape and colour side by side with artificial flowers and stuffed birds. This house belonged to the Lelands. They had bought it in less prosperous days, and having altered it according to their taste and the need of their growing welfare could not decide to leave it.

Sherman was an occasional caller at the Lelands, and had certainly a liking, though not a very deep one, for Margaret. As yet he knew little more about her than that she wore the most fascinating hats, that the late Lord Lytton[12] was her favourite author, and that she hated frogs. It is clear that she did not know that a French writer on magic says the luxurious and extravagant hate frogs because they are cold, solitary, and dreary.[13] Had she done so, she would have been more cautious about revealing her tastes.

For the rest, John Sherman was forgetting the town of Ballah. He corresponded indeed with Mary Carton, but his laborious letter-writing made his letters fewer and fewer. Sometimes, too, he heard from Howard, who had a curacy at Glasgow and was on indifferent terms with his parishioners. They objected to his way of conducting the services. His letters were full of it. He would not give in, he said, whatever happened. His conscience was involved.

II

One afternoon Mrs. Leland called on Mrs. Sherman. She very often called—this fat, sentimental woman, moving in the midst of a cloud of scent. The day was warm, and she carried her too elaborate and heavy dress as a large caddis-fly drags its case with much labour and patience. She sat down on the sofa with obvious relief, leaning so heavily among the cushions that a clothes-moth fluttered out of an antimacassar, to be knocked down and crushed by Mrs. Sherman, who was very quick in her movements.

As soon as she found her breath, Mrs. Leland began a long history of her sorrows. Her daughter Margaret had been jilted and was in despair, had taken to her bed with every resolution to die, and was growing paler and paler. The hard-hearted man, though she knew he had heard, did not relent. She knew he had heard because her daughter had told his sister all about it, and his sister had no heart, because she said it was temper that ailed Margaret, and she was a little vixen, and that if she had not flirted with everybody the engagement would never have been broken off. But Mr. Sims had no heart clearly, as Miss Marriot and Mrs. Eliza Taylor, her daughter's friends, said, when they heard, and Lock, the butler, said the same too, and Mary Young, the house-maid, said so too—and she knew all about it, for Margaret used to read his letters to her often when having her hair brushed.

'She must have been very fond of him,' said Mrs. Sherman.

'She is so romantic, my dear,' answered Mrs. Leland, with a sigh. 'I am afraid she takes after an uncle on her father's side, who wrote poetry and wore a velvet jacket and ran away with an Italian countess who used to get drunk. When I married Mr. Leland people said he was not worthy of me, and that I was throwing myself away—and he in business, too! But Margaret is so romantic. There was Mr. Walters, a gentleman-farmer, and Simpson who had a jeweller's shop—I never approved of him!—and Mr. Samuelson, and the Hon. William Scott. She tired of them all except the Hon. William Scott, who tired of her because someone told him she put belladonna in her eyes[14]—and it is not true; and now there is Mr. Sims!' She then cried a little, and allowed herself to be consoled by Mrs. Sherman.

'You talk so intelligently and are so well informed,' she said at parting. 'I have made a very pleasant call,' and the caddis-worm toiled upon its way, arriving in time at other cups of tea.

III

The day after Mrs. Leland's call upon his mother, John Sherman, returning home after his not very lengthy day in the office, saw Margaret coming towards him. She had a lawn-tennis racket under her arm, and was walking slowly on the shady side of the road. She was a pretty girl with quite irregular features, who though not really more than pretty, had so much manner, so much of an air, that every one called her a beauty: a trefoil with the fragrance of a rose.

'Mr. Sherman,' she cried, coming smiling to meet him, 'I have been ill, but could not stand the house any longer. I am going to the Square to play tennis. Will you come with me?'

'I am a bad player,' he said.

'Of course you are,' she answered; 'but you are the only person under a hundred to be found this afternoon. How dull life is!' she continued, with a sigh. 'You heard how ill I have been? What do you do all day?'

'I sit at a desk, sometimes writing, and sometimes, when I get lazy, looking up at the flies. There are fourteen on the plaster of the ceiling over my head. They died two winters ago. I sometimes think to have them brushed off, but they have been there so long now I hardly like to.'

'Ah! you like them,' she said, 'because you are accustomed to them. In most cases there is not much more to be said for our family affections, I think.'

'In a room close at hand,' he went on, 'there is, you know, Uncle Michael, who never speaks.'

'Precisely. You have an uncle who never speaks; I have a mother who never is silent. She went to see Mrs. Sherman the other day. What did she say to her?'

'Nothing.'

'Really! What a dull thing existence is!'—this with a great sigh. 'When the Fates are weaving our web of life some mischievous goblin always runs off with the dyepot.[15] Everything is dull and grey. Am I looking a little pale? I have been so very ill.'

'A little bit pale, perhaps,' he said, doubtfully.

The Square gate brought them to a stop. It was locked, but she had the key. The lock was stiff, but turned easily for John Sherman.

'How strong you are,' she said.

It was an iridescent evening of spring. The leaves of the bushes had still their faint green. As Margaret darted about at the tennis, a red feather in her cap seemed to rejoice with its wearer. Everything was at once gay and tranquil. The whole world had that unreal air it assumes at beautiful moments, as though it might vanish at a touch like an iridescent soap-bubble.

After a little Margaret said she was tired, and, sitting

on a garden-seat among the bushes, began telling him the plots of novels lately read by her. Suddenly she cried: 'The novel-writers were all serious people like you. They are so hard on people like me. They always make us come to a bad end. They *say* we are always acting, acting, acting; and what else do you serious people do? You act before the world. I think, do you know, *we* act before ourselves. All the old foolish kings and queens in history were like us. They laughed and beckoned and went to the block for no very good purpose. I daresay the headsmen were like you.'

'We would never cut off so pretty a head.'

'Oh, yes, you would—you would cut off mine to-morrow.' All this she said vehemently, piercing him with her bright eyes. 'You would cut off my head to-morrow,' she repeated, almost fiercely; 'I tell you you would.'

Her departure was always unexpected, her moods changed with so much rapidity. 'Look!' she said, pointing where the clock on St. Peter's church showed above the bushes. 'Five minutes to five. In five minutes my mother's tea-hour. It is like growing old. I go to gossip. Good-bye.'

The red feather shone for a moment among the bushes and was gone.

IV

The next day and the day after, Sherman was followed by those bright eyes. When he opened a letter at his desk they seemed to gaze at him from the open paper, and to watch him from the flies upon the ceiling. He was even a worse clerk than usual.

One evening he said to his mother, 'Miss Leland has beautiful eyes.'

'My dear, she puts belladonna in them.'

'What a thing to say!'

'I know she does, though her mother denies it.'

'Well, she is certainly beautiful,' he answered.

'My dear, if she has an attraction for you, I don't want to discourage it. She is rich as girls go nowadays; and one woman has one fault, another another: one's untidy, one fights with her servants, one fights with her friends, another has a crabbed tongue when she talks of them.'

Sherman became again silent, finding no fragment of romance in such a discourse.

In the next week or two he saw much of Miss Leland. He met her almost every evening on his return from the office, walking slowly, her racket under her arm. They played tennis much and talked more. Sherman began to play tennis in his dreams. Miss Leland told him all about herself, her friends, her inmost feelings; and yet every day he knew less about her. It was not merely that saying everything she said nothing, but that continually there came through her wild words the sound of the mysterious flutes and viols of that unconscious nature which dwells so much nearer to woman than to man. How often do we not endow the beautiful and candid with depth and mystery not their own? We do not know that we but hear in their voices those flutes and viols playing to us of the alluring secret of the world.

Sherman had never known in early life what is called first love, and now, when he had passed thirty, it came to him—that love more of the imagination than of either the senses or affections: it was mainly the eyes that followed him.

It is not to be denied that as this love grew serious it grew mercenary. Now active, now latent, the notion had long been in Sherman's mind, as we know, that he should marry money. A born lounger, riches tempted him greatly. When those eyes haunted him from the fourteen flies on the ceiling, he would say, 'I should be rich; I should have a house in the country; I should hunt and shoot, and have a garden and three gardeners; I should leave this abominable office.' Then the eyes became even more beautiful. It was a new kind of belladonna.

He shrank a little, however, from choosing even this pleasant pathway. He had planned many futures for himself and learnt to love them all. It was this that had made him linger on at Ballah for so long, and it was this that now kept him undecided. He would have to give up the universe for a garden and three gardeners. How sad it was to make substantial even the best of his dreams. How hard it was to submit to that decree which compels every step we take in life to be a death in the imagination. How difficult it was to be so enwrapped in this one new hope as not to hear the lamentations that were going on in dim corners of his mind.

One day he resolved to propose. He examined himself in the glass in the morning; and for the first time in his life smiled to see how good-looking he was. In the evening before leaving the office he peered at himself in the mirror over the mantlepiece in the room where customers were received. The sun was blazing through the window full on his face. He did not look so well. Immediately all courage left him.

That evening he went out after his mother had gone to bed and walked far along the towing-path of the Thames.[16] A faint mist half covered away the houses and factory chimneys on the further side; beside him a band of osiers swayed softly, the deserted and full river lapping their stems. He looked on all these things with foreign eyes. He had no sense of possession. Indeed it seemed to him that everything in London was owned by too many to be owned by anyone. Another river that he did seem to possess flowed through his memory with all its familiar sights—boys riding in the stream to the saddle-girths, fish leaping, water-flies raising their small ripples, a swan asleep, the wallflowers growing on the red brick of the margin. He grew very sad. Suddenly a shooting star, fiery and vagabond, leaped from the darkness. It brought his mind again in a moment to Margaret Leland. To marry her, he thought, was to separate himself from the old life he loved so well.

Crossing the river at Putney[17], he hurried homewards among the market-gardens. Nearing home, the streets were deserted, the shops closed. Where King Street joins the Broadway, entirely alone with itself, in the very centre of the road a little black cat was leaping after its shadow.

'Ah!' he thought, 'it would be a good thing to be a little black cat. To leap about in the moonlight and sleep in the sunlight, and catch flies, to have no hard tasks to do or hard decisions to come to, to be simple and full of animal spirits.'

At the corner of Bridge Road was a coffee-stall, the only sign of human life. He bought some cold meat and flung it to the little black cat.

V

Some more days went by. At last, one day, arriving at the Square somewhat earlier than usual, and sitting down to wait for Margaret on the seat among the bushes, he noticed the pieces of a torn-up letter lying about. Beside him on the seat was a pencil, as though someone had been writing there and left it behind them. The pencil-lead was worn very short. The letter had been torn up, perhaps in a fit of impatience.

In a half-mechanical way he glanced over the scraps. On one of them he read: 'MY DEAR ELIZA,—What an incurable gossip my mother is. You heard of my misfortune. I nearly died——' Here he had to search among the scraps; at last he found one that seemed to follow. 'Perhaps you will hear news from me soon. There is a handsome young man who pays me attention, and——' Here another piece had to be found. 'I would take him though he had a face like the man in the moon, and limped like the devil at the theatre. Perhaps I am a little in love. Oh! friend of my heart—' Here it broke off again. He was interested, and searched the grass and the bushes for fragments. Some had been blown to quite a distance. He got together several sentences now. 'I will not spend another winter with my mother for anything. All this is, of course, a secret. I had to tell somebody; secrets are bad for my health. Perhaps it will all come to nothing.' Then the letter went off into dress, the last novel the writer had read, and so forth. A Miss Sims, too, was mentioned, who had said some unkind thing of the writer.

Sherman was greatly amused. It did not seem to him wrong to read—we do not mind spying on one of the crowd, any more than on the personages of literature. It never occurred to him that he, or any friend of his, was concerned in these pencil scribblings.

Suddenly he saw this sentence: 'Heigho! your poor

Margaret is falling in love again; condole with her, my dear.'

He started. The name 'Margaret,' the mention of Miss Sims, the style of the whole letter, all made plain the authorship. Very desperately ashamed of himself, he got up and tore each scrap of paper into still smaller fragments and scattered them far apart.

That evening he proposed and was accepted.

VI

For several days there was a new heaven and a new earth. Miss Leland seemed suddenly impressed with the seriousness of life. She was gentleness itself; and as Sherman sat on Sunday mornings in his pocket-handkerchief of a garden under the one tree, with its smoky stem, watching the little circles of sunlight falling from the leaves like a shower of new sovereigns, he gazed at them with a longer and keener joy than heretofore—a new heaven and a new earth, surely!

Sherman planted and dug and raked this pocket-handkerchief of a garden most diligently, rooting out the docks and dandelions and mouse-ear and the patches of untimely grass. It was the point of contact between his new life and the old. It was far too small and unfertile and shaded-in to satisfy his love of gardener's experiments and early vegetables. Perforce this husbandry was too little complex for his affections to gather much round plant and bed. His garden in Ballah used to touch him like the growth of a young family. Now he was content to satisfy his barbaric sense of colour; right round were planted alternate hollyhock and sunflower, and behind them scarlet-runners showed their inch-high cloven shoots.

One Sunday it occurred to him to write to his friends on the matter of his engagement. He numbered them over. Howard, one or two less intimate, and Mary Carton. At that name he paused; he would not write just yet.

VII

One Saturday there was a tennis party. Miss Leland devoted herself all day to a young Foreign Office clerk. She played tennis with him, talked with him, drank lemonade with him, had neither thoughts nor words for anyone else. John Sherman was quite happy. Tennis was always a bore, and now he was not called upon to play. It had not struck him there was occasion for jealousy.

As the guests were dispersing, his betrothed came to him. Her manner seemed strange.

'Does anything ail you, Margaret?' he asked, as they left the Square.

'Everything,' she answered, looking about her with ostentatious secrecy. 'You are a most annoying person. You have no feeling; you have no temperament; you are quite the most stupid creature I was ever engaged to.'

'What is wrong with you?' he asked, in bewilderment.

'Don't you see,' she replied, with a broken voice, 'I flirted all day with that young clerk? You should have nearly killed me with jealousy. You do not love me a bit! There is no knowing what I might do!'

'Well, you know,' he said, 'it was not right of you. People might say, "Look at John Sherman; how furious he must be!" To be sure, I wouldn't be furious a bit; but then they'd go about saying I was. It would not matter, of course; but you know it is not right of you.' 'It is no use pretending you have feeling. It is all that miserable little town you come from, with its sleepy old shops and its sleepy old society. I would give up loving you this minute,' she added, with a caressing look, 'if you had not that beautiful bronzed face. I will improve you. To-morrow evening you must come to the opera.' Suddenly she changed the subject. 'Do you see that little fat man coming out of the Square and staring at me? I was engaged to him once. Look at the four old ladies behind him, shaking their bonnets at me. Each has some story about me, and it will be all the same in a hundred years.'

After this he had hardly a moment's peace. She kept him continually going to theatres, operas, parties. These last were an especial trouble; for it was her wont to gather about her an admiring circle to listen to her extravagancies, and he was no longer at the age when we enjoy audacity for its own sake.

VIII

Gradually those bright eyes of his imagination, watching him from letters and from among the fourteen flies on the ceiling, had ceased to be centres of peace. They seemed like two whirlpools, wherein the order and quiet of his life were absorbed hourly and daily. He still thought sometimes of the country house of his dreams and of the garden and the three gardeners, but somehow they had lost half their charm.

He had written to Howard and some others, and commenced, at last, a letter to Mary Carton. It lay unfinished on his desk; a thin coating of dust was gathering upon it.

Mrs. Leland called continually on Mrs. Sherman. She sentimentalized over the lovers, and even wept over them; each visit supplied the household with conversation for a week.

Every Sunday morning—his letter-writing time— Sherman looked at his uncompleted letter. Gradually it became plain to him he could not finish it. It had never seemed to him he had more than friendship for Mary Carton, yet somehow it was not possible to tell her of this love-affair.

The more his betrothed troubled him the more he thought about the unfinished letter. He was a man standing at the cross roads.

Whenever the wind blew from the south he remembered his friend, for that is the wind that fills the heart with memory.

One Sunday he removed the dust from the face of the letter almost reverently, as though it were the dust from the wheels of destiny. But the letter remained unfinished.

IX

One Wednesday in June Sherman arrived home an hour earlier than usual from his office, as his wont was the first Wednesday in every month, on which day his mother was at home to her friends. They had not many callers. To-day there was no one as yet but a badly-dressed old lady his mother had picked up he knew not where. She had been looking at his photograph album, and recalling names and dates from her own prosperous times. As she went out Miss Leland came in. She gave the old lady in passing a critical look that made the poor creature very conscious of a threadbare mantle, and went over to Mrs. Sherman, holding out both hands. Sherman, who knew all his mother's peculiarities, noticed on her side a slight coldness; perhaps she did not altogether like this beautiful dragon-fly.

'I have come,' said Miss Leland, 'to tell John that he must learn to paint. Music and society are not enough. There is nothing like art to give refinement.' Then turning to John Sherman—'My dear, I will make you quite different. You are a dreadful barbarian, you know.'

'What ails me, Margaret?'

'Just look at that necktie! Nothing shows a man's cultivation like his necktie! Then your reading! You never read anything but old books nobody wants to talk about. I will lend you three everyone has read this month. You really must acquire small talk and change your necktie.'

Presently she noticed the photograph-book lying open on a chair.

'Oh!' she cried, 'I must have another look at John's beauties.'

It was a habit of his to gather all manner of pretty faces. It came from incipient old bachelorhood, perhaps.

Margaret criticised each photograph in turn with, 'Ah! she looks as if she had some life in her!' or 'I do not like your sleepy eyelids,' or some such phrase. The mere relations were passed by without a word. One face occurred several times—a quiet face. As Margaret came on this one for the third time, Mrs. Sherman, who seemed a little resentful about something, said: 'That is his friend, Mary Carton.'

'He told me about her. He has a book she gave him. So that is she? How interesting! I pity these poor country people. It must be hard to keep from getting stupid.'

'My friend is not at all stupid,' said Sherman.

'Does she speak with a brogue? I remember you told me she was very good. It must be difficult to keep from talking platitudes when one is very good.'

'You are quite wrong about her. You would like her very much,' he replied.

'She is one of those people, I suppose, who can only talk about their relatives, or their families, or about their friends' children: how this one has got the whooping-cough, and this one is getting well of the measles!' She kept swaying one of the leaves between her finger and thumb impatiently. 'What a strange way she does her hair; and what an ugly dress!'

'You must not talk that way about her—she is my great friend.'

'Friend! friend!' she burst out. 'He thinks I will believe in friendship between a man and a woman!'

She got up, and said, turning round with an air of changing the subject, 'Have you written to your friends about our engagement? You had not done so when I asked you lately.'

'I have.'

'All?'

'Well, not all.'

'Your great friend, Miss——what do you call her?'

'Miss Carton. I have not written to her.'

She tapped impatiently with her foot.

'They were really old companions—that is all,' said Mrs. Sherman, wishing to mend matters. 'They were both readers; that brought them together. I never much fancied her. Yet she was well enough as a friend, and helped, maybe, with reading, and the gardening, and his good bringing-up, to keep him from the idle young men of the neighbourhood.'

'You must make him write and tell her at once—you must, you must!' almost sobbed out Miss Leland.

'I promise,' he answered.

Immediately returning to herself, she cried, 'If I were in her place I know what I would like to do when I got the letter. I know who I would like to kill!'—this with a laugh as she went over and looked at herself in the mirror on the mantlepiece.

THIRD PART

JOHN SHERMAN REVISITS BALLAH

I

The others had gone, and Sherman was alone in the drawing-room by himself, looking through the window. Never had London seemed to him so like a reef whereon he was cast away. In the Square the bushes were covered with dust; some sparrows were ruffling their feathers on the side-walk; people passed, continually disturbing them. The sky was full of smoke. A terrible feeling of solitude in the midst of a multitude oppressed him. A portion of his life was ending. He thought that soon he would be no longer a young man, and now, at the period when the desire of novelty grows less, was coming the great change of his life. He felt he was of those whose granaries are in the past. And now this past would never renew itself. He was going out into the distance as though with strange sailors in a strange ship.

He longed to see again the town where he had spent his childhood: to see the narrow roads and mean little shops. And perhaps it would be easier to tell her who had been the friend of so many years of this engagement in his own person than by letter. He wondered why it was so hard to write so simple a thing.

It was his custom to act suddenly on his decisions. He had not made many in his life. The next day he announced at the office that he would be absent for three or four days. He told his mother he had business in the country. His betrothed met him on the way to the terminus, as he was walking, bag in hand, and asked where he was going. 'I am going on business to the country,' he said, and blushed. He was creeping away like a thief.

II

He arrived in the town of Ballah by rail, for he had avoided the slow cattle-steamer and gone by Dublin. It was the forenoon, and he made for the Imperial Hotel to wait till four in the evening, when he would find Mary Carton in the school-house, for he had timed his journey so as to arrive on Thursday, the day of the children's practice.

As he went through the streets his heart went out to every familiar place and sight: the rows of tumble-down thatched cottages; the slated roofs of the shops; the women selling gooseberries; the river bridge; the high walls of the garden where it was said the gardener used to see the ghost of a former owner in the shape of a rabbit; the street corner no child would pass at nightfall for fear of the headless soldier; the deserted flour-store; the wharves covered with grass. All these he watched with Celtic devotion, that devotion carried to the ends of the world by the Celtic exiles, and since old time surrounding their journeyings with rumour of plaintive songs.

He sat in the window of the Imperial Hotel, now full of guests. He did not notice any of them. He sat there meditating, meditating. Grey clouds covering the town with flying shadows rushed by like the old and dishevelled eagles that Maeldune saw hurrying towards the waters of life.[18] Below in the street passed by country people, townspeople, travellers, women with baskets, boys driving donkeys, old men with sticks; sometimes he recognized a face or was recognized himself, and welcomed by some familiar voice.

'You have come home a handsomer gentleman than your father, Misther John, and he was a neat figure of a man, God bless him!' said the waiter, bringing him his lunch; and in truth Sherman had grown handsomer for these years away. His face and gesture had more of dignity, for on the centre of his nature life had dropped a pinch of experience.

At four he left the hotel and waited near the schoolhouse till the children came running out. One or two of the elder ones he recognized but turned away.

III

Mary Carton was locking the harmonium as he went in. She came to meet him with a surprised and joyful air.

'How often I have wished to see you! When did you come? How well you remembered my habits to know where to find me. My dear John, how glad I am to see you!'

'You are the same as when I left, and this room is the same, too.'

'Yes,' she answered, 'the same, only I have had some new prints hung up—prints of fruits and leaves and birdnests. It was only done last week. When people choose pictures and poems for children they choose out such domestic ones. I would not have any of the kind; children are such undomestic animals. But, John, I am so glad to see you in this old school-house again. So little has changed with us here. Some have died and some have been married, and we are all a little older and the trees a little taller.'

'I have come to tell you I am going to be married.'

She became in a moment perfectly white, and sat down as though attacked with faintness. Her hand on the edge of the chair trembled.

Sherman looked at her, and went on in a bewildered, mechanical way: 'My betrothed is a Miss Leland. She has a good deal of money. You know my mother always wished me to marry some one with money. Her father, when alive, was an old client of Sherman and Saunders. She is much admired in society.' Gradually his voice became a mere murmur. He did not seem to know that he was speaking. He stopped entirely. He was looking at Mary Carton.

Everything around him was as it had been some three years before. The table was covered with cups and the floor with crumbs. Perhaps the mouse pulling at a crumb under the table was the same mouse as on that other evening. The only difference was the brooding daylight of summer and the ceaseless chirruping of the sparrows in the ivy outside. He had a confused sense of having lost his way. It was just the same feeling he had known as a child, when one dark night he had taken a wrong turning, and instead of arriving at his own house, found himself at a landmark he knew was miles from home.

A moment earlier, however difficult his life, the issues were always definite; now suddenly had entered the obscurity of another's interest.

Before this it had not occurred to him that Mary

Carton had any stronger feeling for him than warm friendship.

He began again, speaking in the same mechanical way: 'Miss Leland lives with her mother near us. She is very well educated and very well connected, though she has lived always among business people.'

Miss Carton, with a great effort, had recovered her composure.

'I congratulate you,' she said. 'I hope you will be always happy. You came here on some business for your firm, I suppose? I believe they have some connection with the town still.'

'I only came here to tell you I was going to be married.'

'Do you not think it would have been better to have written?' she said, beginning to put away the children's tea-things in a cupboard by the fireplace.

'It would have been better,' he answered, drooping his head.

Without a word, locking the door behind them, they went out. Without a word they walked the grey streets. Now and then a woman or a child curtseyed as they passed. Some wondered, perhaps, to see these old friends so silent. At the rectory they bade each other good-bye.

'I hope you will be always happy,' she said. 'I will pray for you and your wife. I am very busy with the children and old people, but I shall always find a moment to wish you well in. Good-bye now.'

They parted; the gate in the wall closed behind her. He stayed for a few moments looking up at the tops of the trees and bushes showing over the wall, and at the house a little way beyond. He stood considering his problem—her life, his life. His, at any rate, would have incident and change; hers would be the narrow existence of a woman who, failing to fulfil the only abiding wish she has ever formed, seeks to lose herself in routine—mournfulest of things on this old planet.

This had been revealed: he loved Mary Carton, she loved him. He remembered Margaret Leland, and murmured she did well to be jealous. Then all her contemptuous words about the town and its inhabitants came into his mind. Once they made no impression on him, but now the sense of personal identity having been disturbed by this sudden revelation, alien as they were to his way of thinking, they began to press in on him. Mary, too, would have agreed with them, he thought; and might it be that at some distant time weary monotony in abandonment would have so weighed down the spirit of Mary Carton that she would be merely one of the old and sleepy whose dulness filled the place like a cloud?

He went sadly towards the hotel; everything about him, the road, the sky, the feet wherewith he walked seeming phantasmal and without meaning.

He told the waiter he would leave by the first train in the morning. 'What! and you only just come home?' the man answered. He ordered coffee and could not drink it. He went out and came in again immediately. He went down into the kitchen and talked to the servants. They told him of everything that had happened since he had gone. He was not interested, and went up to his room. 'I must go home and do what people expect of me; one must be careful to do that.'

Through all the journey home his problem troubled him. He saw the figure of Mary Carton perpetually passing through a round of monotonous duties. He saw his own life among aliens going on endlessly, wearily.

From Holyhead[19] to London his fellow-travellers were a lady and her three young daughters, the eldest about twelve. The smooth faces shining with well-being became to him ominous symbols. He hated them. They were symbolic of the indifferent world about to absorb him, and of the vague something that was dragging him inch by inch from the nook he had made for himself in the chimney-corner. He was at one of those dangerous moments when the sense of personal identity is shaken, when one's past and present seem about to dissolve partnership. He sought refuge in memory, and counted over every word of Mary's he could remember. He forgot the present and the future. 'Without love,' he said to himself, 'we would be either gods or vegetables.'

The rain beat on the window of the carriage. He began to listen; thought and memory became a blank; his mind was full of the sound of rain-drops.

FOURTH PART

THE REV. WILLIAM HOWARD

I

After his return to London Sherman for a time kept to himself, going straight home from his office, moody and self-absorbed, trying not to consider his problem —her life, his life. He often repeated to himself, 'I must do what people expect of me. It does not rest with me now—my choosing time is over.' He felt that whatever way he turned he would do a great evil to himself and others. To his nature all sudden decisions were difficult, and so he kept to the groove he had entered upon. It did not even occur to him to do otherwise. He never thought of breaking this engagement off and letting people say what they would. He was bound in hopelessly by a chain of congratulations.

A week passed slowly as a month. The wheels of the cabs and carriages seemed to be rolling through his mind. He often remembered the quiet river at the end of his garden in the town of Ballah. How the weeds swayed there, and the salmon leaped! At the week's end came a note from Miss Leland, complaining of his neglecting her so many days. He sent a rather formal answer, promising to call soon. To add to his other troubles, a cold east wind arose and made him shiver continually.

One evening he and his mother were sitting silent, the one knitting, the other half-asleep. He had been writing letters and was now in a reverie. Round the walls were one or two drawings, done by him at school. His mother had got them framed. His eyes were fixed on a drawing of a stream and some astonishing cows. A few days ago he had found an old sketch-book for children among some forgotten papers, which taught how to draw a horse by making three ovals for the basis of his body, one lying down in the middle, two standing up at each end for flank and chest, and how to draw a cow by basing its body on a square. He kept trying to fit squares into the cows. He was half inclined to take them out of their frames and retouch on this new principle. Then he began somehow to remember the child with the swollen face who threw a stone at the dog the day he resolved to leave home first. Then some other image came. His problem moved before him in a disjointed way. He was dropping asleep. Through his reverie came the click, click of his mother's needles. She had found some London children to knit for. He was at that marchland between waking and dreaming where our thoughts begin to have a life of their own—the region where art is nurtured and inspiration born.

He started, hearing something sliding and rustling, and looked up to see a piece of cardboard fall from one end of the mantelpiece, and, driven by a slight gust of air, circle into the ashes under the grate.

'Oh,' said his mother, 'that is the portrait of the *locum tenens*.' She still spoke of the Rev. William Howard by the name she had first known him by. 'He is always being photographed. They are all over the house, and I, an old woman, have not had one taken all my life. Take it out with the tongs.' Her son, after some poking in the ashes, for it had fallen far back, brought out a somewhat dusty photograph. 'That,' she continued, 'is one he sent us two or three months ago. It has been lying in the letter-rack since.'

'He is not so spick-and-span-looking as usual,' said Sherman, rubbing the ashes off the photograph with his sleeve.

'By the by,' his mother replied, 'he has lost his parish, I hear. He is very mediæval, you know, and he lately preached a sermon to prove that children who die unbaptized are lost. He had been reading up the subject and was full of it. The mothers turned against him, not being so familiar with St. Augustine as he was.[20] There were other reasons in plenty too. I wonder that anyone can stand that monkeyish fantastic family.'

As the way is with so many country-bred people, the world for her was divided up into families rather than individuals.

While she was talking, Sherman, who had returned to his chair, leant over the table and began to write hurriedly. She was continuing her denunciation when he interrupted with: 'Mother, I have just written this letter to him:—

' "My Dear Howard:
' "Will you come and spend the autumn with us? I hear you are unoccupied just now. I am engaged to be married, as you know; it will be a long engagement. You will like my betrothed. I hope you will be great friends.
' "Yours expectantly,
' "John Sherman." '

'You rather take me aback,' she said.

'I really like him,' he answered. 'You were always prejudiced against the Howards. Forgive me, but I really want very much to have him here.'

'Well, if you like him, I suppose I have no objection.'

'I do like him. He is very clever,' said her son, 'and knows a great deal. I wonder he does not marry. Do you not think he would make a good husband?—for you must admit he is sympathetic.'

'It is not difficult to sympathize with everyone if you have no true principles and convictions.'

Principles and convictions were her names for that strenuous consistency attained without trouble by men and women of few ideas.

'I am sure you will like him better,' said the other, 'when you see more of him.'

'Is that photograph quite spoilt?' she answered.

'No; there was nothing on it but ashes.'

'That is a pity, for one less would be something.'

After this they both became silent, she knitting, he gazing at the cows browsing at the edge of their stream, and trying to fit squares into their bodies; but now a smile played about his lips.

Mrs. Sherman looked a little troubled. She would not object to any visitor of her son's, but quite made up her mind in no manner to put herself out to entertain the Rev. William Howard. She was puzzled as well. She did not understand the suddenness of this invitation. They usually talked over things for weeks.

II

Next day his fellow-clerks noticed a decided improvement in Sherman's spirits. He had a lark-like cheerfulness and alacrity breaking out at odd moments. When evening came he called, for the first time since his return, on Miss Leland. She scolded him for having answered her note in such a formal way, but was sincerely glad to see him return to his allegiance. We have said he had sometimes, though rarely, a talkative fit. He had one this evening. The last play they had been to, the last party, the picture of the year, all in turn he glanced at. She was delighted. Her training had not been in vain. Her barbarian was learning to chatter. This flattered her a deal.

'I was never engaged,' she thought, 'to a more interesting creature.'

When he had risen to go, Sherman said: 'I have a friend coming to visit me in a few days; you will suit each other delightfully. He is very mediæval.'

'Do tell me about him; I like everything mediæval.'

'Oh,' he cried, with a laugh, 'his mediævalism is not in your line. He is neither a gay troubadour nor a wicked knight. He is a High Church curate.'

'Do not tell me anything more about him,' she answered; 'I will try to be civil to him, but you know I never liked curates. I have been an agnostic for many years. You, I believe, are orthodox.'

As Sherman was on his way home he met a fellow-clerk, and stopped him with: 'Are you an agnostic?'

'No. Why, what is that?'

'Oh, nothing! Good-bye,' he made answer, and hurried on his way.

III

The letter reached the Rev. William Howard at the right moment, arriving as it did in the midst of a crisis in his fortunes. In the course of a short life he had lost many parishes. He considered himself a martyr, but was considered by his enemies a clerical coxcomb. He had a habit of getting his mind possessed with some strange opinion, or what seemed so to his parishioners, and of preaching it while the notion lasted in the most startling way. The sermon on unbaptized children was an instance. It was not so much that he thought it true as that it possessed him for a day. It was not so much the thought as his own relation to it that allured him. Then, too, he loved what appeared to his parishioners to be the most unusual and dangerous practices. He put candles on the altar and crosses in unexpected places. He delighted in the intricacies of High Church costume, and was known to recommend confession and prayers for the dead.

Gradually the anger of his parishioners would increase. The rector, the washerwoman, the labourers, the squire, the doctor, the school-teachers, the shoemakers, the butchers, the seamstresses, the local journalist, the master of the hounds, the innkeeper, the veterinary surgeon, the magistrate, the children making mud pies, all would be filled with one dread—popery. Then he would fly for consolation to his little circle of the faithful, the younger ladies, who still repeated his fine sentiments and saw him in their imaginations standing perpetually before a wall covered with tapestry and holding a crucifix in some constrained and ancient attitude. At last he would have to go, feeling for his parishioners a gay and lofty disdain, and for himself that reverent approbation one gives to the captains who lead the crusade of ideas against those who merely sleep and eat. An efficient crusader he certainly was—too efficient, indeed, for his efficiency gave to all his thoughts a certain over-completeness and isolation, and a kind of hardness to his mind. His intellect was like a musician's instrument with no sounding-board. He could think carefully and cleverly, and even with originality, but never in such a way as to make his thoughts an allusion to something deeper than themselves. In this he was the reverse of poetical, for poetry is essentially a touch from behind a curtain.

This conformation of his mind helped to lead him into all manner of needless contests and to the loss of this last parish among much else. Did not the world exist for the sake of these hard, crystalline thoughts, with which he played as with so many bone spilikins, delighting in his own skill? and were not all who disliked them merely—the many?

In this way it came about that Sherman's letter reached Howard at the right moment. Now, next to a new parish, he loved a new friend. A visit to London meant many. He had found he was, on the whole, a success at the beginning of friendships.

He at once wrote an acceptance in his small and beautiful handwriting, and arrived shortly after his letter. Sherman, on receiving him, glanced at his neat and shining boots, the little medal at the watch-chain and the well-brushed hat, and nodded as though in answer to an inner query. He smiled approval at the slight elegant figure in its black clothes, at the satiny hair, and at the face, mobile as moving waters.

For several days the Shermans saw little of their guest. He had friends everywhere to turn into enemies and acquaintances to turn into friends. His days passed in visiting, visiting, visiting. Then there were theatres and churches to see, and new clothes to be bought, over which he was as anxious as a woman. Finally he settled down.

He passed his mornings in the smoking-room. He asked Sherman's leave to hang on the walls one or two religious pictures, without which he was not happy, and to place over the mantelpiece, under the pipe-rack, an ebony crucifix. In one corner of the room he laid a rug neatly folded for covering his knees on chilly days, and on the table a small collection of favourite books—a curious and carefully-chosen collection, in which Cardinal Newman and Bourget, St. Chrysostom and Flaubert lived together in perfect friendship.[21]

Early in his visit Sherman brought him to the Lelands. He was a success. The three—Margaret, Sherman, and Howard—played tennis in the Square. Howard was a good player, and seemed to admire Margaret. On the way home Sherman once or twice laughed to himself. It was like the clucking of a hen with a brood of chickens. He told Howard, too, how wealthy Margaret was said to be.

After this Howard always joined Sherman and Margaret at the tennis. Sometimes, too, after a little, on days when the study seemed dull and lonely, and the unfinished essay on St. Chrysostom more than usually laborious, he would saunter towards the Square before his friend's arrival, to find Margaret now alone, now with an acquaintance or two. About this time also press of work, an unusual thing with him, began to delay Sherman in town half-an-hour after his usual time. In the evenings they often talked of Margaret—Sherman frankly and carefully, as though in all anxiety to describe her as she was; and Howard with some enthusiasm: 'She has a religious vocation,' he said once, with a slight sigh.

Sometimes they played chess—a game that Sherman had recently become devoted to, for he found it drew him out of himself more than anything else.

Howard now began to notice a curious thing. Sherman grew shabbier and shabbier, and at the same time more and more cheerful. This puzzled him, for he had noticed that he himself was not cheerful when shabby, and did not even feel upright and clever when his hat was getting old. He also noticed that when Sherman was talking to him he seemed to be keeping some thought to himself. When he first came to know him long ago in Ballah he had noticed occasionally the same thing, and set it down to a kind of suspiciousness and over-caution, natural to one who lived in such an out-of-the-way place. It seemed more persistent now, however. 'He is not well-trained,' he thought; 'he is half a peasant. He has not the brilliant candour of the man of the world.'

All this while the mind of Sherman was clucking continually over its brood of thoughts. Ballah was being constantly suggested to him. The grey corner of a cloud slanting its rain upon Cheapside [22] called to mind by some remote suggestion the clouds rushing and falling in cloven surf on the seaward steep of a mountain north of Ballah. A certain street-corner made him remember an angle of the Ballah fish-market. At night a lantern, marking where the road was fenced off for mending, made him think of a tinker's cart, with its swing-can of burning coals, that used to stop on market days at the corner of Peter's Lane at Ballah. Delayed by a crush in the Strand, [23] he heard a faint trickling of water near by; it came from a shop window where a little water-jet balanced a wooden ball upon its point. The sound suggested a cataract with a long Gaelic name, that leaped crying into the Gate of the Winds at Ballah.[24] Wandering among these memories a footstep went to and fro continually, and the figure of Mary Carton moved among them like a phantom. He was set dreaming a whole day by walking down one Sunday morning to the border of the Thames—a few hundred yards from his house— and looking at the osier-covered Chiswick eyot.[25] It made him remember an old day-dream of his. The source of the river that passed his garden at home was a certain wood-bordered and islanded lake, whither in childhood he had often gone blackberry-gathering. At the further end was a little islet called Innisfree.[26] Its rocky centre, covered with many bushes, rose some forty feet above the lake. Often when life and its difficulties had seemed to him like the lessons of some elder boy given to a younger by mistake, it had seemed good to dream of going away to that islet and building a wooden hut there and burning a few years out, rowing to and fro, fishing, or lying on the island slopes by day, and listening at night to the ripple of the water and the quivering of the bushes—full always of unknown creatures—and going out at morning to see the island's edge marked by the feet of birds.

These pictures became so vivid to him that the world about him—that Howard, Margaret, his mother even —began to seem far off. He hardly seemed aware of anything they were thinking and feeling. The light that dazzled him flowed from the vague and refracting regions of hope and memory; the light that made Howard's feet unsteady was ever the too-glaring lustre of life itself.

IV

On the evening of the 20th of June, after the blinds had been pulled down and the gas lighted, Sherman was playing chess in the smoking-room, right hand against left. Howard had gone out with a message to the Lelands. He would often say, 'Is there any message I can deliver for you? I know how lazy you are, and will save you the trouble.' A message was always found for him. A pile of books lent for Sherman's improvement went home one by one.

'Look here,' said Howard's voice in the doorway, 'I have been watching you for some time. You are cheating the red men most villainously. You are forcing them to make mistakes that the white men may win. Why, a few such games would ruin any man's moral nature.'

He was leaning against the doorway, looking, to Sherman's not too critical eyes, an embodiment of all that was self-possessed and brilliant. The great care with which he was dressed and his whole manner seemed to say: 'Look at me; do I not combine perfectly the zealot with the man of the world?' He seemed excited to-night. He had been talking at the Lelands, and talking well, and felt that elation which brings us many thoughts.

'My dear Sherman,' he went on, 'do cease that game. It is very bad for you. There is nobody alive who is honest enough to play a game of chess fairly out—right hand against left. We are so radically dishonest that we even cheat ourselves. We can no more play chess than we can think altogether by ourselves with security. You had much better play with me.'

'Very well, but you will beat me; I have not much practice,' replied the other.

They reset the men and began to play. Sherman relied

most upon his bishops and queen. Howard was fondest of the knights. At first Sherman was the attacking party, but in his characteristic desire to scheme out his game many moves ahead, kept making slips, and at last had to give up, with his men nearly all gone and his king hopelessly cornered. Howard seemed to let nothing escape him. When the game was finished he leant back in his chair and said, as he rolled a cigarette: 'You do not play well.' It gave him satisfaction to feel his proficiency in many small arts. 'You do not do any of these things at all well,' he went on, with an insolence peculiar to him when excited. 'You have been really very badly brought up and stupidly educated in that intolerable Ballah. They do not understand there any, even the least, of the arts of life; they only believe in information. Men who are compelled to move in the great world, and who are also cultivated, only value the personal acquirements—self-possession, adaptability, how to dress well, how even to play tennis decently—you would be not so bad at that, by the by, if you practised—or how to paint or write effectively. They know that it is better to smoke one's cigarette with a certain charm of gesture than to have by heart all the encyclopedias. I say this not merely as a man of the world, but as a teacher of religion. A man when he rises from the grave will take with him only the things that he is in himself. He will leave behind the things that he merely possesses, learning and information not less than money and high estate. They will stay behind with his house and his clothes and his body. A collection of facts will no more help him than a collection of stamps. The learned will not get into heaven as readily as the flute-player, or even as the man who smokes a cigarette gracefully. Now, you are not learned, but you have been brought up almost

as badly as if you were. In that wretched town they told
you that education was to know that Russia is bounded
on the north by the Arctic Sea, and on the west by the
Baltic Ocean, and that Vienna is situated on the Danube,
and that William the Third came to the throne in the
year 1688.[27] They have never taught you any personal
art. Even chess-playing might have helped you at the
day of judgment.'

'I am really not a worse chess-player than you. I am
only more careless.'

There was a slight resentment in Sherman's voice.
The other noticed it, and said, changing his manner from
the insolent air of a young beauty to a self-depreciatory
one, which was wont to give him at times a very genuine
charm: 'It is really a great pity, for you Shermans are a
deep people, much deeper than we Howards. We are
like moths or butterflies, or rather rapid rivulets, while
you and yours are deep pools in the forest where the
beasts go to drink. No! I have a better metaphor. Your
mind and mine are two arrows. Yours has got no feathers, and mine has no metal on the point. I don't know
which is most needed for right conduct. I wonder where
we are going to strike earth. I suppose it will be all right
some day when the world has gone by and they have
collected all the arrows into one quiver.'

He went over to the mantelpiece to hunt for a match,
as his cigarette had gone out. Sherman had lifted a corner
of the blind and was gazing over the roofs shining from
a recent shower, and thinking how on such a night as
this he had sat with Mary Carton by the rectory fire
listening to the rain without and talking of the future
and of the training of village children.

'Have you seen Miss Leland in her last new dress
from Paris?' said Howard, making one of his rapid tran-

sitions. 'It is very rich in colour, and makes her look a little pale, like Saint Cecilia.[28] She is wonderful as she stands by the piano, a silver cross round her neck. We have been talking about you. She complains to me. She says you are a little barbarous. You seem to look down on style, and sometimes—you must forgive me—even on manners, and you are quite without small talk. You must really try and be worthy of that beautiful girl, with her great soul and religious genius. She told me quite sadly, too, that you are not improving.'

'No,' said Sherman, 'I am not going forward; I am at present trying to go sideways like the crabs.'

'Be serious,' answered the other. 'She told me these things with the most sad and touching voice. She makes me her confidant, you know, in many matters, because of my wide religious experience. You must really improve yourself. You must paint or something.'

'Well, I will paint or something.'

'I am quite serious, Sherman. Try and be worthy of her, a soul as gentle as Saint Cecilia's.'

'She is very wealthy,' said Sherman. 'If she were engaged to you and not to me you might hope to die a bishop.'

Howard looked at him in a mystified way and the conversation dropped. Presently Howard got up and went to his room, and Sherman, resetting the chessboard, began to play again, and, letting longer and longer pauses of reverie come between his moves, played far into the morning, cheating now in favour of the red men, now in favour of the white.

V

The next afternoon Howard found Miss Leland sitting, reading in an alcove in her drawing-room, between a stuffed parroquet and a blue De Morgan jar.[29] As he was shown in he noticed, with a momentary shock, that her features were quite commonplace. Then she saw him, and at once seemed to vanish wrapped in an exulting flame of life. She stood up, flinging the book on to the seat with some violence.

'I have been reading the "Imitation of Christ,"[30] and was just feeling that I should have to become a theosophist or a socialist, or go and join the Catholic Church, or do something. How delightful it is to see you again! How is my savage getting on? It is so good of you to try and help me to reform him.'

They talked on about Sherman, and Howard did his best to console her for his shortcomings. Time would certainly improve her savage. Several times she gazed at him with those large dark eyes of hers, of which the pupils to-day seemed larger than usual. They made him feel dizzy and clutch tightly the arm of his chair. Then she began to talk about her life since childhood—how they got to the subject he never knew—and made a number of those confidences which are so dangerous because so flattering. To love—there is nothing else worth living for; but then men are so shallow. She had never found a nature deep as her own. She would not pretend that she had not often been in love, but never had any heart rung back to her the true note. As she spoke her face quivered with excitement. The exulting flame of life seemed spreading from her to the other things in the room. To Howard's eyes it seemed as though the bright pots and stuffed birds and plush curtains began to glow with a light not of this world—to glimmer like the strange and chaotic colours the mystic Blake imagined upon the scaled serpent of Eden.[31] The light seemed gradually to dim his past and future, and to make pale his good resolves. Was it not in itself that which all men are seeking, and for which all else exists? He leant forward and took her hand, timidly and doubtingly. She did not draw it away. He leant nearer and kissed her on the forehead. She gave a joyful cry, and, casting her arms round his neck, burst out, 'Ah! you—and I. We were made for each other. I hate Sherman. He is an egotist. He is a beast. He is selfish and foolish.' Releasing one of her arms she struck the seat with her hand, excitedly, and went on, 'How angry he will be! But it serves him right! How badly he is dressing. He does not know anything about anything. But you—you—I knew you were meant for me the moment I saw you.'

That evening Howard flung himself into a chair in the empty smoking-room. He lighted a cigarette; it went out. Again he lighted it; again it went out. 'I am a traitor—and that good, stupid fellow, Sherman, never to be jealous!' he thought. 'But then, how could I help it? And, besides, it cannot be a bad action to save her from a man she is so much above in refinement and feeling.' He was getting into good-humour with himself. He got up and went over and looked at the photograph of Raphael's Madonna, which he had hung over the mantelpiece.[32] 'How like Margaret's are her big eyes!'

VI

The next day when Sherman came home from his office he saw an envelope lying on the smoking-room table. It contained a letter from Howard, saying that he had gone away, and that he hoped Sherman would forgive his treachery, but that he was hopelessly in love with Miss Leland, and that she returned his love.

Sherman went downstairs. His mother was helping the servant to set the table.

'You will never guess what has happened,' he said. 'My affair with Margaret is over.'

'I cannot pretend to be sorry, John,' she replied. She had long considered Miss Leland among accepted things, like the chimney-pots on the roof, and submitted, as we do, to any unalterable fact, but had never praised her or expressed liking in any way. 'She puts belladonna in her eyes, and is a vixen and a flirt, and I dare say her wealth is all talk. But how did it happen?'

Her son was, however, too excited to listen.

He went upstairs and wrote the following note:

'MY DEAR MARGARET:
  'I congratulate you on a new conquest. There is no end to your victories. As for me, I bow myself out with many sincere wishes for your happiness, and remain,
                              'Your friend,
                              'JOHN SHERMAN.'

Having posted this letter he sat down with Howard's note spread out before him, and wondered whether there was anything mean and small-minded in neatness—he himself was somewhat untidy. He had often thought so before, for their strong friendship was founded in a great measure on mutual contempt, but now immediately added, being in good-humour with the world, 'He is much cleverer than I am. He must have been very industrious at school.'

A week went by. He made up his mind to put an end to his London life. He broke to his mother his resolve to return to Ballah. She was delighted, and at once began to pack. Her old home had long seemed to her a kind of lost Eden,³³ wherewith she was accustomed to contrast the present. When, in time, this present had grown into the past it became an Eden in turn. She was always ready for a change, if the change came to her in the form of a return to something old. Others place their ideals in the future; she laid hers in the past.

The only one this momentous resolution seemed to surprise was the old and deaf servant. She waited with ever-growing impatience. She would sit by the hour wool-gathering on the corner of a chair with a look of bewildered delight. As the hour of departure came near she sang continually in a cracked voice.

Sherman, a few days before leaving, was returning for the last time from his office when he saw, to his surprise, Howard and Miss Leland carrying each a brown-paper bundle. He nodded good-humouredly, meaning to pass on.

'John,' she said, 'look at this brooch William gave me—a ladder leaning against the moon and a butterfly climbing up it.³⁴ Is it not sweet? We are going to visit the poor.'

'And I,' he said, 'am going to catch eels. I am leaving town.'

He made his excuses, saying he had no time to wait, and hurried off. She looked after him with a mournful glance, strange in anybody who had exchanged one lover for another more favoured.

'Poor fellow,' murmured Howard, 'he is broken-hearted.'

'Nonsense,' answered Miss Leland, somewhat snappishly.

FIFTH PART

JOHN SHERMAN RETURNS TO BALLAH

I

This being the homeward trip, SS. *Lavinia* carried no cattle, but many passengers. As the sea was smooth and the voyage near its end, they lounged about the deck in groups. Two cattle-merchants were leaning over the taffrail smoking. In appearance they were something between betting-men and commercial travellers. For years they had done all their sleeping in steamers and trains. A short distance from them a clerk from Liverpool, with a consumptive cough, walked to and fro, a little child holding his hand. Shortly he would be landed in a boat putting off from the shore for the purpose. He had come hoping that his native air of Teeling Head[35] would restore him. The little child was a strange contrast—her cheeks ruddy with perfect health. Further forward, talking to one of the crew, was a man with a red face and slightly unsteady step. In the companion-house was a governess, past her first youth, very much afraid of sea-sickness. She had brought her luggage up and heaped it round her to be ready for landing. Sherman sat on a pile of cable looking out over the sea. It was just noon; SS. *Lavinia*, having passed by Tory and Rathlin, was approaching the Donegal cliffs.[36] They were covered by a faint mist, which made them loom even vaster than they were. To westward the sun shone on a perfectly blue sea. Seagulls came out of the mist and

67

plunged into the sunlight, and out of the sunlight and plunged into the mist. To the westward gannets were striking continually, and a porpoise showed now and then, his fin and back gleaming in the sun. Sherman was more perfectly happy than he had been for many a day, and more ardently thinking. All nature seemed full of a Divine fulfilment. Everything fulfilled its law— fulfilment that is peace, whether it be for good or for evil, for evil also has its peace, the peace of the birds of prey. Sherman looked from the sea to the ship and grew sad. Upon this thing, crawling slowly along the sea, moved to and fro many mournful and slouching figures. He looked from the ship to himself and his eyes filled with tears. On himself, on these moving figures, hope and memory fed like flames.

Again his eyes gladdened, for he knew he had found his present. He would live in his love and the day as it passed. He would live that his law might be fulfilled. Now, was he sure of this truth—the saints on the one hand, the animals on the other, live in the moment as it passes. Thitherward had his days brought him. This was the one grain they had ground. To grind one grain is sufficient for a lifetime.

II

A few days later Sherman was hurrying through the town of Ballah. It was Saturday, and he passed down through the marketing country people, and the old women with baskets of cakes and gooseberries and long pieces of sugarstick shaped like walking-sticks, and called by children 'Peggie's leg.'

Now, as two months earlier, he was occasionally

recognized and greeted, and, as before, went on without knowing, his eyes full of unintelligent sadness because the mind was making merry afar. They had the look we see in the eyes of animals and dreamers. Everything had grown simple, his problem had taken itself away. He was thinking what he would say to Mary Carton. Now they would be married, they would live in a small house with a green door and new thatch, and a row of beehives under a hedge. He knew where just such a house stood empty. The day before he and his mother had discussed, with their host of the Imperial Hotel, this question of houses. They knew the peculiarities of every house in the neighbourhood, except two or three built while they were away. All day Sherman and his mother had gone over the merits of the few they were told were empty. She wondered why her son had grown so unpractical. Once he was so easily pleased—the row of beehives and the new thatch did not for her settle the question. She set it all down to Miss Leland and the plays, and the singing, and the belladonna, and remembered with pleasure how many miles of uneasy water lay between the town of Ballah and these things.

She did not know what else besides the row of beehives and the new thatch her son's mind ran on as he walked among the marketing country people, and the gooseberry sellers, and the merchants of 'Peggie's leg,' and the boys playing marbles in odd corners, and the men in waistcoats with flannel sleeves driving carts, and the women driving donkeys with creels of turf or churns of milk. Just now she was trying to remember whether she used to buy her wool for knitting at Miss Peter's or from Mrs. Macallough's at the bridge. One or other sold it a halfpenny a skein cheaper. She never knew what went on inside her son's mind, she had always her own fish to fry. Blessed are the unsympathetic. They preserve their characters in an iron bottle while the most of us poor mortals are going about the planet vainly searching for any kind of a shell to contain us, and evaporating the while.

Sherman began to mount the hill to the vicarage. He was happy. Because he was happy he began to run. Soon the steepness of the hill made him walk. He thought about his love for Mary Carton. Seen by the light of this love everything that had happened to him was plain now. He had found his centre of unity. His childhood had prepared him for this love. He had been solitary, fond of favourite corners of fields, fond of going about alone, unhuman like the birds and the leaves, his heart empty. How clearly he remembered his first meeting with Mary. They were both children. At a school treat they watched the fire-balloon ascend, and followed it a little way over the fields together. What friends they became, growing up together, reading the same books, thinking the same thoughts!

As he came to the door and pulled at the great hanging iron bell-handle, the fire-balloon reascended in his heart, surrounded with cheers and laughter.

III

He kept the servant talking for a moment or two before she went for Miss Carton. The old rector, she told him, was getting less and less able to do much work. Old age had come almost suddenly upon him. He seldom moved from the fireside. He was getting more and more absent-minded. Once lately he had brought his umbrella into the reading-desk. More and more did he leave all things to his children—to Mary Carton and her younger sisters.

When the servant had gone, Sherman looked round the somewhat gloomy room. In the window hung a canary in a painted cage. Outside was a narrow piece of shaded ground between the window and the rectory wall. The laurel and holly bushes darkened the window a good deal. On a table in the centre of the room were evangelistic books with gilded covers. Round the mirror over the mantelpiece were stuck various parish announcements, thrust between the glass and the gilding. On a small side-table was a copper ear-trumpet.

How familiar everything seemed to Sherman! Only the room seemed smaller than it did three years before, and close to the table with the ear-trumpet, at one side of the fireplace before the arm-chair, was a new threadbare patch in the carpet.

Sherman recalled how in this room he and Mary Carton had sat in winter by the fire, building castles in the air for each other. So deeply meditating was he that she came in and stood unnoticed beside him.

'John,' she said at last, 'it is a great pleasure to see you so soon again. Are you doing well in London?'

'I have left London.'

'Are you married, then? You must introduce me to your wife.'

'I shall never be married to Miss Leland.'

'What?'

'She has preferred another—my friend William Howard. I have come here to tell you something, Mary.' He went and stood close to her and took her hand tenderly. 'I have always been very fond of you. Often in

London, when I was trying to think of another kind of life, I used to see this fireside and you sitting beside it, where we used to sit and talk about the future. Mary— Mary,' he held her hand in both his—'you will be my wife?'

'You do not love me, John,' she answered, drawing herself away. 'You have come to me because you think it your duty. I have had nothing but duty all my life.'

'Listen,' he said. 'I was very miserable; I invited Howard to stay with us. One morning I found a note on the smoking-room table to say that Margaret had accepted him, and I have come here to ask you to marry me. I never cared for anyone else.'

He found himself speaking hurriedly, as though anxious to get the words said and done with. It now seemed to him that he had done ill in this matter of Miss Leland. He had not before thought of it—his mind had always been busy with other things. Mary Carton looked at him wonderingly.

'John,' she said at last, 'did you ask Mr. Howard to stay with you on purpose to get him to fall in love with Miss Leland, or to give you an excuse for breaking off your engagement, as you knew he flirted with everyone?'

'Margaret seems very fond of him. I think they are made for each other,' he answered.

'Did you ask him to London on purpose?'

'Well, I will tell you,' he faltered. 'I was very miserable. I had drifted into this engagement I don't know how. Margaret glitters and glitters and glitters, but she is not of my kind. I suppose I thought, like a fool, I should marry someone who was rich. I found out soon that I loved nobody but you. I got to be always thinking of you and of this town. Then I heard that Howard had lost his curacy, and asked him up. I just left them alone and did not go near Margaret much. I knew they were made for each other. Do not let us talk of them,' he continued, eagerly. 'Let us talk about the future. I will take a farm and turn farmer. I dare say my uncle will not give me anything when he dies because I have left his office. He will call me a ne'er-do-weel, and say I would squander it. But you and I—we will get married, will we not? We will be very happy,' he went on, pleadingly. 'You will still have your charities, and I shall be busy with my farm. We will surround ourselves with a wall. The world will be on the outside, and on the inside we and our peaceful lives.'

'Wait,' she said; 'I will give you your answer,' and going into the next room returned with several bundles of letters. She laid them on the table; some were white and new, some slightly yellow with time.

'John,' she said, growing very pale, 'here are all the letters you ever wrote me from your earliest boyhood.' She took one of the large candles from the mantelpiece, and, lighting it, placed it on the hearth. Sherman wondered what she was going to do with it. 'I will tell you,' she went on, 'what I had thought to carry to the grave unspoken. I have loved you for a long time. When you came and told me you were going to be married to another I forgave you, for man's love is like the wind, and I prayed that God might bless you both.' She leant down over the candle, her face pale and contorted with emotion. 'All these letters after that grew very sacred. Since we were never to be married they grew a portion of my life, separated from everything and everyone— a something apart and holy. I re-read them all, and arranged them in little bundles according to their dates, and tied them with thread. Now I and you—we have nothing to do with each other any more.'

She held the bundle of letters in the flame. He got up from his seat. She motioned him away imperiously. He looked at the flame in a bewildered way. The letters fell in little burning fragments about the hearth. It was all like a terrible dream. He watched those steady fingers hold letter after letter in the candle flame, and watched the candle burning on like a passion in the grey daylight of universal existence. A draught from under the door began blowing the ash about the room. The voice said—

'You tried to marry a rich girl. You did not love her, but knew she was rich. You tired of her as you tire of so many things, and behaved to her most wrongly, most wickedly and treacherously. When you were jilted you came again to me and to the idleness of this little town. We had all hoped great things of you. You seemed good and honest.'

'I loved you all along,' he cried. 'If you would marry me we would be very happy. I loved you all along,' he repeated—this helplessly, several times over. The bird shook a shower of seed on his shoulder. He picked one of them from the collar of his coat and turned it over in his fingers mechanically. 'I loved you all along.'

'You have done no duty that came to you. You have tired of everything you should cling to; and now you have come to this little town because here is idleness and irresponsibility.'

The last letter lay in ashes on the hearth. She blew out the candle, and replaced it among the photographs on the mantelpiece, and stood there as calm as a portion of the marble.

'John, our friendship is over—it has been burnt in the candle.'

He started forward, his mind full of appeals half-stifled with despair, on his lips gathered incoherent words: 'She will be happy with Howard. They were made for each other. I slipped into it. I always thought I should marry someone who was rich. I never loved anyone but you. I did not know I loved you at first. I thought about you always. You are the root of my life.'

Steps were heard outside the door at the end of a passage. Mary Carton went to the door and called. The steps turned and came nearer. With a great effort Sherman controlled himself. The door opened, and a tall, slight girl of twelve came into the room. A strong smell of garden mould rose from a basket in her hands. Sherman recognized the child who had given him tea that evening in the schoolhouse three years before.

'Have you finished weeding the carrots?' said Mary Carton.

'Yes, Miss.'

'Then you are to weed the small bed under the pear-tree by the tool-house. Do not go yet, child. This is Mr. Sherman. Sit down a little.'

The child sat down on the corner of a chair with a scared look in her eyes. Suddenly she said—

'Oh, what a lot of burnt paper!'

'Yes; I have been burning some old letters.'

'I think,' said John, 'I will go now.' Without a word of farewell he went out, almost groping his way.

He had lost the best of all the things he held dear.

Twice he had gone through the fire. The first time worldly ambition left him; the second, love. An hour before the air had been full of singing and peace that was resonant like joy. Now he saw standing before his Eden the angel with the flaming sword.[37] All the hope he had ever gathered about him had taken itself off, and the naked soul shivered.

IV

The road under his feet felt gritty and barren. He hurried away from the town. It was late afternoon. Trees cast bands of shadow across the road. He walked rapidly as if pursued. About a mile to the west of the town he came on a large wood bordering the road and surrounding a deserted house. Some local rich man once lived there, now it was given over to a caretaker who lived in two rooms in the back part. Men were at work cutting down trees in two or three parts of the wood. Many places were quite bare. A mass of ruins—a covered well, and the wreckage of castle wall—that had been roofed with green for centuries, lifted themselves up, bare as anatomies.[38] The sight intensified, by some strange sympathy, his sorrow, and he hurried away as from a thing accursed of God.

The road led to the foot of a mountain, topped by a cairn supposed in popular belief to be the grave of Maeve, Mab of the fairies, and considered by antiquarians to mark the place where certain prisoners were executed in legendary times as sacrifices to the moon.[39]

He began to climb the mountain. The sun was on the rim of the sea. It stayed there without moving, for as he ascended he saw an ever-widening circle of water.

He threw himself down upon the cairn. The sun sank under the sea. The Donegal headlands mixed with the surrounding blue. The stars grew out of heaven. Sometimes he got up and walked to and fro. Hours passed. The stars, the streams down in the valley, the wind moving among the boulders, the various unknown creatures rustling in the silence—all these were contained within themselves, fulfilling their law, content to be alone, content to be with others, having the peace of God or the peace of the birds of prey. He only did not fulfil his law; something that was not he, that was not nature, that was not God, had made him and her he loved its tools. Hope, memory, tradition, conformity, had been laying waste their lives. As he thought this the night seemed to crush him with its purple foot. Hour followed hour. At midnight he started up, hearing a faint murmur of clocks striking the hour in the distant town. His face and hands were wet with tears, his clothes saturated with dew.

He turned homeward, hurriedly flying from the terrible firmament. What had this glimmering and silence to do with him—this luxurious present? He belonged to the past and the future. With pace somewhat slackened, because of the furze, he came down into the valley. Along the northern horizon moved a perpetual dawn, travelling eastward as the night advanced. Once, as he passed a marsh near a lime-kiln, a number of small birds rose chirruping from where they had been clinging among the reeds. Once, standing still for a moment where two roads crossed on a hill-side, he looked out over the dark fields. A white stone rose in the middle of a field, a score of yards in front of him. He knew the place well; it was an ancient burying-ground. He looked at the stone, and suddenly filled by the terror of the darkness children feel, began again his hurried walk.

He re-entered Ballah by the southern side. In passing he looked at the rectory. To his surprise a light burned in the drawing-room. He stood still. The dawn was brightening towards the east, but all round him was darkness, seeming the more intense to his eyes for their being fresh from the unshaded fields. In the midst of this darkness shone the lighted window. He went over to the gate and looked in. The room was empty. He was about to turn away when he noticed a white figure standing close to the gate. The latch creaked and the gate moved slowly on its hinges.

'John,' said a trembling voice, 'I have been praying, and a light has come to me. I wished you to be ambitious—to go away and do something in the world. You did badly, and my poor pride was wounded. You do not know how much I had hoped from you; but it was all pride—all pride and foolishness. You love me. I ask no more. We need each other; the rest is with God.'

She took his hand in hers, and began caressing it. 'We have been shipwrecked. Our goods have been cast into the sea.' Something in her voice told of the emotion that divides the love of woman from the love of man. She looked upon him whom she loved as full of a helplessness that needed protection, a reverberation of the feeling of the mother for the child at the breast.

DHOYA

DHOYA

I

Long ago, before the earliest stone of the Pyramids was laid, before the Bo tree of Buddha unrolled its first leaf, before a Japanese had painted on a temple wall the horse that every evening descended and trampled the rice-fields, before the ravens of Thor had eaten their first worm together, there lived a man of giant stature and of giant strength named Dhoya.[1] One evening Fomorian galleys had entered the Bay of the Red Cataract, now the Bay of Ballah, and there deserted him.[2] Though he rushed into the water and hurled great stones after them, they were out of reach. From earliest childhood the Fomorians had held him captive and compelled him to toil at the oar, but when his strength had come his fits of passion made him a terror to all on board. Sometimes he would tear the seats of the galley from under the rowers, and drive the rowers up into the shrouds, where they would cling until the passion left him. 'The demons,' they said, 'have made him their own.' So they enticed him on shore, he having on his head a mighty stone pitcher to fill with water, and deserted him.

When the last sail had dropped over the rim of the world, he rose from where he had flung himself down on the sands and hurried through the forest eastward. After a time he reached that lake among the mountains where in later times Diarmuid drove down four stakes and made thereon a platform with four flags in the centre for a hearth, and placed over all a roof of wicker and

skins, and hid his Grania, islanded thereon.[3] Still
eastward he went, what is now Bulben on one side,
Cope's mountain on the other, until at last he threw
himself at full length in a deep cavern and slept.[4]
Henceforward he made this cavern his lair, issuing forth
to hunt the deer or the bears or the mountain oxen.
Slowly the years went by, his fits of fury growing more
and more frequent, though there was no one but his
own shadow to rave against. When his fury was on him
even the bats and owls, and the brown frogs that crept
out of the grass at twilight, would hide themselves—
even the bats and owls and the brown frogs. These he
had made his friends, and let them crawl and perch about
him, for at times he would be very gentle, and they too
were sullen and silent—the outcasts from they knew not
what. But most of all, things placid and beautiful feared
him. He would watch for hours, hidden in the leaves,
to reach his hand out slowly and carefully at last, and
seize and crush some glittering halcyon.

Slowly the years went by and human face he never
saw, but sometimes, when the gentle mood was on him
and it was twilight, a presence seemed to float invisibly
by him and sigh softly, and once or twice he awoke
from sleep with the sensation of a finger having rested
for a moment on his forehead, and would mutter a
prayer to the moon that glimmered through the door
of his cave before turning to sleep again. 'O moon,' he
would say, 'that wanderest in the blue cave of the sky,
more white than the beard of Partholan,[5] whose years
were five hundred, sullen and solitary, sleeping only on
the floor of the sea: keep me from the evil spirits of the
islands of the lake southward beyond the mountains,
and the evil spirits of the caves northward beyond the

mountains, and the evil spirits who wave their torches
by the mouth of the river eastward beyond the valley,
and the evil spirits of the pools westward beyond the
mountains, and I will offer you a bear and a deer in full
horn, O solitary of the cave divine, and if any have done
you wrong I will avenge you.'

Gradually, however, he began to long for this mysterious touch.

At times he would make journeys into distant parts,
and once the mountain bulls gathered together, proud
of their overwhelming numbers and their white horns,
and followed him with great bellowing westward, he
being laden with their tallest, well-nigh to his cave, and
would have gored him, but, pacing into a pool of the
sea to his shoulders, he saw them thunder away, losing
him in the darkness. The place where he stood is called
Pooldhoya to this day.[6]

So the years went slowly by, and ever deeper and
deeper came his moodiness, and more often his fits of
wrath. Once in his gloom he paced the forests for miles,
now this way, now that, until, returning in the twilight,
he found himself standing on a cliff southward of the
lake that was southward of the mountains. The moon
was rising. The sound of the swaying of reeds floated
from beneath, and the twittering of the flocks of reed-
wrens who love to cling on the moving stems. It was
the hour of votaries. He turned to the moon, then hurriedly gathered a pile of leaves and branches, and making
a fire cast thereon wild strawberries and the fruit of the
quicken-tree. As the smoke floated upwards a bar of
faint purple clouds drifted over the moon's face—a re-
fusal of the sacrifice. Hurrying through the surrounding
woods he found an owl sleeping in the hollow of a tree,

and returning cast him on the fire. Still the clouds gathered. Again he searched the woods. This time it was a
badger that he cast among the flames. Time after time
he came and went, sometimes returning immediately
with some live thing, at others not till the fire had almost
burnt itself out. Deer, wild swine, birds, all to no purpose. Higher and higher he piled the burning branches,
the flames and the smoke waved and circled like the lash
of a giant's whip. Gradually the nearer islands passed
the rosy colour on to their more distant brethren. The
reed-wrens of the furthest reed beds disturbed amid their
sleep must have wondered at the red gleam reflected in
each other's eyes. Useless his night-long toil; the clouds
covered the moon's face more and more, until, when
the long fire-lash was at its brightest, they drowned her
completely in a surge of unbroken mist. Raging against
the fire he scattered with his staff the burning branches,
and trampled in his fury the sacrificial embers beneath
his feet. Suddenly a voice in the surrounding darkness
called him softly by name. He turned. For years no
articulate voice had sounded in his ears. It seemed to
rise from the air just beneath the verge of the precipice.
Holding by a hazel bush he leaned out, and for a moment
it seemed to him the form of a beautiful woman floated
faintly before him, but changed as he watched to a little
cloud of vapour; and from the nearest of the haunted
islands there came assuredly a whiff of music. Then
behind him in the forest said the voice, 'Dhoya, my
beloved.' He rushed in pursuit; something white was
moving before him. He stretched out his hand; it was
only a mass of white campion trembling in the morning
breeze, for an ashen morning was just touching the mists
on the eastern mountains. Beginning suddenly to trem-

ble with supernatural fear Dhoya turned homewards. Everything was changed; dark shadows seemed to come and go, and elfin chatter to pass upon the breeze. But when he reached the shelter of the pine woods all was still as of old. He slackened his speed. Those solemn pine-trees soothed him with their vast unsociability— many and yet each one alone. Once or twice, when in some glade further than usual from its kind arose a pine-tree larger than the rest, he paused with bowed head to mutter an uncouth prayer to that dark outlaw. As he neared his cave and came from the deep shade into the region of mountain-ash and hazel,[7] the voices seemed again to come and go, and the shadows to circle round him, and once a voice said, he imagined, in accents faint and soft as falling dew, 'Dhoya, my beloved.' But a few yards from the cave all grew suddenly silent.

II

Slower and slower he went, with his eyes on the ground, bewildered by all that was happening. A few feet from the cave he stood still, counting aimlessly the round spots of light made by the beams slanting through trees that hid with their greenness, as in the centre of the sea, that hollow rock. As over and over he counted them, he heard, first with the ear only, then with the mind also, a footstep going to and fro within the cave. Lifting his eyes he saw the same figure seen on the cliff—the figure of a woman, beautiful and young. Her dress was white, save for a border of feathers dyed the fatal red of the spirits.[8] She had arranged in one corner the spears, and in the other the brushwood and branches used for the fire, and spread upon the ground the skins, and now began pulling vainly at the great stone pitcher of the Fomorians.

Suddenly she saw him and with a burst of laughter flung her arms around his neck, crying, 'Dhoya, I have left my world far off. My people—on the floor of the lake they are dancing and singing, and on the islands of the lake; always happy, always young, always without change. I have left them for thee, Dhoya, for they cannot love. Only the changing, and moody, and angry, and weary can love. I am beautiful; love me, Dhoya. Do you hear me? I left the places where they dance, Dhoya, for thee!' For long she poured out a tide of words, he answering at first little, then more and more as she melted away the silence of so many inarticulate years; and all the while she gazed on him with eyes, no ardour could rob of the mild and mysterious melancholy that watches us from the eyes of animals—sign of unhuman reveries.

Many days passed over these strangely-wedded ones. Sometimes when he asked her, 'Do you love me?' she would answer, 'I do not know, but I long for your love endlessly.' Often at twilight, returning from hunting, he would find her bending over a stream that flowed near to the cave, decking her hair with feathers and reddening her lips with the juice of a wild berry.

He was very happy secluded in that deep forest. Hearing the faint murmurs of the western sea, they seemed to have outlived change. But Change is everywhere, with the tides and the stars fastened to her wheel. Every blood-drop in their lips, every cloud in the sky, every leaf in the world changed a little, while they brushed back their hair and kissed. All things change save only the fear of change. And yet for his hour Dhoya was happy and as full of dreams as an old man or an infant—for dreams wander nearest to the grave and the cradle.

Once, as he was returning home from hunting, by the northern edge of the lake, at the hour when the owls cry to each other, 'It is time to be abroad,' and the last flutter of the wind has died away, leaving under every haunted island an image legible to the least hazel branch, there suddenly stood before him a slight figure, at the edge of the narrow sand-line, dark against the glowing water. Dhoya drew nearer. It was a man leaning on his spear-staff, on his head a small red cap. His spear was slender and tipped with shining metal; the spear of Dhoya of wood, one end pointed and hardened in the fire. The red-capped stranger silently raised that slender spear and thrust at Dhoya, who parried with his pointed staff.

For a long while they fought. The last vestige of sunset passed away and the stars came out. Underneath them the feet of Dhoya beat up the ground, but the feet of the other as he rushed hither and thither, matching his agility with the mortal's mighty strength, made neither shadow nor footstep on the sands. Dhoya was wounded, and growing weary a little, when the other leaped away, and, crouching down by the water, began: 'You have carried away by some spell unknown the most beautiful of our bands—you who have neither laughter nor singing. Restore her, Dhoya, and go free.' Dhoya answered him no word, and the other rose and again thrust at him with the spear. They fought to and fro upon the sands until the dawn touched with olive the distant sky, and then his anger-fit, long absent, fell on Dhoya, and he closed with his enemy and threw

him, and put his knee on his chest and his hands on his
throat, and would have crushed all life out of him, when
lo! he held beneath his knee no more than a bundle of
reeds.

Nearing home in the early morning he heard the
voice he loved, singing:

> Full moody is my love and sad,
>   His moods bow low his sombre crest,
> I hold him dearer than the glad,
>   And he shall slumber on my breast.
>
> My love hath many an evil mood,
>   Ill words for all things soft and fair,
> I hold him dearer than the good,
>   My fingers feel his amber hair.
>
> No tender wisdom floods the eyes
>   That watch me with their suppliant light—
> I hold him dearer than the wise,
>   And for him make me wise and bright.[9]

And when she saw him she cried, 'An old mortal song
heard floating from a tent of skin, as we rode, I and
mine, through a camping-place at night.' From that day
she was always either singing wild and melancholy
songs or else watching him with that gaze of animal
reverie.

Once he asked, 'How old are you?'

'A thousand years, for I am young.'

'I am so little to you,' he went on, 'and you are so
much to me—dawn, and sunset, tranquillity, and
speech, and solitude.'

'Am I so much?' she said; 'say it many times!' and

her eyes seemed to brighten and her breast heaved with joy.

Often he would bring her the beautiful skins of animals, and she would walk to and fro on them, laughing to feel their softness under her feet. Sometimes she would pause and ask suddenly, 'Will you weep for me when we have parted?' and he would answer, 'I will die then'; and she would go on rubbing her feet to and fro in the soft skin.

And so Dhoya grew tranquil and gentle, and Change seemed still to have forgotten them, having so much on her hands. The stars rose and set watching them smiling together, and the tides ebbed and flowed, bringing mutability to all save them. But always everything changes, save only the fear of Change.

III

One evening as they sat in the inner portion of the cave, watching through the opening the paling of the sky and the darkening of the leaves, and counting the budding stars, Dhoya suddenly saw stand before him the dark outline of him he fought on the lake sand, and heard at the same instant his companion sigh.

The stranger approached a little, and said, 'Dhoya, we have fought heretofore, and now I have come to play chess against thee, for well thou knowest, dear to the perfect warrior after war is chess.'[10]

'I know it,' answered Dhoya.

'And when we have played, Dhoya, we will name the stake.'

'Do not play,' whispered his companion at his side.

But Dhoya, being filled with his anger-fit at the sight of his enemy, answered, 'I will play, and I know well the stake you mean, and I name this for mine, that I may again have my knee on your chest and my hands on your throat, and that you will not again change into a bundle of wet reeds.' His companion lay down on a skin and began to cry a little.

Dhoya felt sure of winning. He had often played in his boyhood, before the time of his anger-fits, with his masters of the galley; and besides, he could always return to his hands and his weapons once more.

Now the floor of the cave was of smooth, white sand, brought from the seashore in his great Fomorian pitcher, to make it soft for his beloved to walk upon; before it had been, as it now is, of rough clay. On this sand the red-capped stranger marked out with his spear-point a chess-board, and marked with rushes, crossed and recrossed each alternate square, fixing each end of the rush in the sand, until a complete board was finished of white and green squares, and then drew from a bag large chessmen of mingled wood and silver. Two or three would have made an armful for a child. Standing each at his end they began to play. The game did not last long. No matter how carefully Dhoya played, each move went against him. At last, leaping back from the board, he cried, 'I have lost!' The two spirits were standing together at the entrance. Dhoya seized his spear, but slowly the figures began to fade, first a star and then the leaves showed through their forms. Soon all had vanished away.

Then, understanding his loss, he threw himself on the ground, and rolling hither and thither, roared like a wild beast. All night long he lay on the ground, and all the next day till nightfall. He had crumbled his staff unconsciously between his fingers into small pieces, and now, full of dull rage, the pointed end of the staff still in his hand, arose and went forth westward. In a ravine of the northern mountain he came on the tracks of wild horses. Soon one passed him fearlessly, knowing nothing of man. He drove the pointed end of the staff deep in the flank, making a great wound, sending the horse rushing with short screams down the mountain. Other horses passed him one by one, driven southward by a cold wind laden with mist, arisen in the night-time. Towards the end of the ravine stood one black and huge, the leader of the herd. Dhoya leaped on his back with a loud cry that sent a raven circling from the neighbouring cliff, and the horse, after vainly seeking to throw him, rushed off towards the north-west, over the heights of the mountains where the mists floated. The moon, clear sometimes of the flying clouds, from low down in the south-east, cast a pale and mutable light, making their shadow rise before them on the mists, as though they pursued some colossal demon, sombre on his black charger. Then leaving the heights they rushed down that valley where, in far later times, Diarmuid hid in a deep cavern his Grania,[11] and passed the stream where Muadhan, their savage servant, caught fish for them on a hook baited with a quicken-berry.[12] On over the plains, on northward, mile after mile, the wild gigantic horse leaping cliff and chasm in his terrible race; on until the mountains of what is now Donegal[13] rose before them—over these among the clouds, driving rain blowing in their faces from the sea, Dhoya knowing not whither he went, or why he rode. On—the stones loosened by the hoofs rumbling down into the valleys—till far in the distance he saw the sea, a thousand feet below him; then, fixing his eyes thereon, and using the spear-point as a goad, he roused his black horse into redoubled speed, until horse and rider plunged headlong into the Western Sea.

Sometimes the cotters on the mountains of Donegal hear on windy nights a sudden sound of horses' hoofs, and say to each other, 'There goes Dhoya.' And at the same hour men say if any be abroad in the valleys they see a huge shadow rushing along the mountain.[14]

APPENDIX

"GANCONAGH'S APOLOGY"

[Yeats doubtless composed this "Apology" in the spring of 1891, after *John Sherman and Dhoya* had been accepted by T. Fisher Unwin for his "Pseudonym Library." It was included in the 1891–92 editions but was not reprinted in the 1908 *Collected Works in Verse & Prose*.]

GANCONAGH'S APOLOGY.

The maker of these stories has been told that he must not bring them to you himself. He has asked me to pretend that I am the author. I am an old little Irish spirit, and I sit in the hedges and watch the world go by. I see the boys going to market driving donkeys with creels of turf, and the girls carrying baskets of apples. Sometimes I call to some pretty face, and we chat a little in the shadow, the apple basket before us, for, as my faithful historian O'Kearney has put it in his now yellow manuscript, I care for nothing in the world but love and idleness.[1] Will not you, too, sit down under the shade of the bushes while I read you the stories? The first I do not care for because it deals with dull persons and the world's affairs, but the second has to do with my own people. If my voice at whiles grows distant and dreamy when I talk of the world's affairs, remember that I have seen all from my hole in the hedge. I hear continually the songs of my own people who dance upon the hill-side, and am content. I have never carried apples or driven turf myself, or if I did it was only in a dream. Nor do my kind use any of man's belongings except the little black pipes which the farmers find now and then when they are turning the sods over with a plough.

GANCONAGH.

EXPLANATORY NOTES TO
[PREFACE]

1. Yeats was twenty-two when he wrote *Dhoya* and began *John Sherman*; the latter was essentially finished when he was twenty-three.
2. As Elizabeth Heine has explained in "W. B. Yeats's Map in His Own Hand," *Biography* 1.3 (Summer 1978), 43:

   The Water-Carrier is Aquarius, Yeats's rising sign. "Saturn's hour" refers to the transit in 1888 of Saturn, that slow-moving planet, through the early degrees of the sign Leo, directly opposite Yeats's ascendant, and then on through a conjunction with Yeats's natal Mars in Leo. Saturn, old Chronos, is by tradition a malefic planet, the time-keeper who makes us work hard and face up to our responsibilities. Ascendants are very sensitive points, and an opposition often a very stressful aspect. To Yeats in 1907, looking back to the tensions of his life in 1888, his difficulties in writing the novel reflected the opposition of Saturn.

   Further, at the precise time of Yeats's birth, "the first degree of Aquarius was rising in the east; directly opposite, setting in the west, was the first degree of Leo. The sun, in Gemini, was well below the western horizon; the moon, below the eastern horizon in Aquarius, was due to rise about midnight. . . . Yeats is within astrological traditions when he interprets these astronomical positions to mean that he would have to work through the moon's reflection to permit the sun to be fully recognized" (letter to Richard J. Finneran, 29 August 1990).
3. Sligo is a town on the northwest coast of Ireland where Yeats spent a substantial part of his childhood, living with his maternal grandparents. In his *History of Sligo, County and Town* (Dublin: Hodges, Figgis, 1882–92), W. G. Wood-Martin explains that "The channel to Sligo crosses an extensive flat called the Bar. The deepest water over it (about 13 feet at low water) is defined by buoys; and within the bar the water deepens to about 20 feet in a good anchorage called Pooldoy, where vessels lie in moderate weather to wait for water to enter the Harbour" (III: 221).
4. Henry Middleton, a cousin of Yeats, lived alone in a supposedly

haunted house called Elsinore at Rosses Point, County Sligo.
Yeats wrote of him in "Three Songs to the One Burden":

> My name is Henry Middleton
> I have a small demesne,
> A small forgotten house that's set
> On a storm-bitten green,
> I scrub its floors and make my bed,
> I cook and change my plate,
> The Post and Garden-boy alone
> Have keys to my old gate.

(*The Poems*, revised edition, ed. Richard J. Finneran [New York:
Macmillan, 1989], p. 329.)

EXPLANATORY NOTES TO
JOHN SHERMAN

1. An actual hotel in Sligo, though no longer in business.
2. Howard is the temporary replacement for the curate.
3. In the Prologue to the opera *Mefistofele* (1868) by the Italian composer Arrigo Boito (1842–1918).
4. William Shakespeare (1564–1616), English dramatist; *Travels in the Interior of Africa* (1799) by the English writer Mungo Park (1771–1806); *Reliques of Ancient English Poetry* (1765), collected by the English writer Thomas Percy (1729–1811).
5. A fine, dyed wool.
6. The Virgin Mary, mother of Christ in the Christian religion.
7. The Sligo Steam Navigation Company, owned by Yeats's grandfather, William Pollexfen (1811–92), offered weekly service between Sligo and Liverpool, using the steamers *Glasgow, Liverpool,* and *Sligo.* Yeats may have taken the name *Lavinia* from a steamer registered in Dublin in 1890. Alternatively, there were many sailing ships of that name, including at least one which occasionally called at Liverpool, departing there, for instance, on 13 July 1889.
8. The river at Liverpool.
9. A district in the west of London.
10. The Cape of Good Hope is at the southern end of Africa; Mozambique is in eastern Africa; Port Said is in Egypt, at one end of the Suez Canal.
11. The Pre-Raphaelite movement in art and literature, which began in England in 1848, derived its aesthetics from the Italian painters before Raphael (1483–1520).
12. Edward George Earle Lytton Bulwer-Lytton (1803–73), English novelist, playwright, and politician.
13. The French writer has not been traced.
14. Atropine, a poisonous drug extracted from the plant belladonna, or deadly nightshade, dilates the pupils of the eyes and was thus used for cosmetic purposes.
15. In classical mythology, the three Fates control the lives of men. Clotho spins the web of life, Lachesis measures it, and Atropos severs it.
16. The Thames is the principal river in London.

17. A district in London, on the south side of the Thames.
18. The reference is to "The Voyage of Maildun," which Yeats would have read in *Old Celtic Romances*, trans. P. W. Joyce (London: David Nutt, 1879). In an episode entitled "The Isle of the Mystic Lake," Maildun and his companions observe an aged eagle undergo a renewal of youth by bathing in a lake: "Meantime the old bird, after the others had left, continued to smooth and plume his feathers till evening; then, shaking his wings, he rose up, and flew three times round the island, as if to try his strength. And now the men observed that he had lost all the appearances of old age: his feathers were thick and glossy, his head was erect and his eye bright, and he flew with quite as much power and swiftness as the others" (p. 161).
19. A small island off the west coast of England, the chief port for passenger service from Dublin.
20. The Christian theologian Saint Augustine (354–430) affirmed the necessity of infant baptism: because of Original Sin, children must be baptised to be eligible for salvation.
21. John Henry Newman (1801–90), English churchman and author; Paul Bourget (1852–1935), French novelist; St. John Chrysostom (ca. 347–407), archbishop of Constantinople; Gustave Flaubert (1821–80), French novelist.
22. A district in the City of London.
23. A street in London.
24. One of the waterfalls which drop from the slope of Ben Bulben into Glencar Lake near Sligo. As described by W. G. Wood-Martin in *History of Sligo, County and Town* (Dublin: Hodges, Figgis, 1882–92), "one of them is called in Irish *Sruth-an-ail-an-ard, i.e.*, the stream against the height, from the singular and deceptive appearance it presents of the reversal of the ordinary laws of hydrology. When the wind blows from one particular point, the water is either driven upwards and back against the mountain, or it is blown outwards from it in a sheet of spray like a pennant" (I: 85–86).
   To my knowledge there is no place-name referring to the Sligo area which can be translated as "Gate of the Winds." There is, however, a gap in the hills opposite Carraroe Church in County Sligo called *Bearna na Gaoithe* ("Gap of the Wind"), known in English as "Windy Gap." This may be referred to in the first line of "Running to Paradise" (*The Poems*, revised edition, ed. Richard J. Finneran [New York: Macmillan, 1989], p. 115).
25. Chiswick is a borough in Middlesex, near London. An "eyot" is a small island.
26. A small island in Lough Gill, County Sligo.
27. William III (1650–1702), king of England, defeated the forces

of James II (1633–1701), the former king, at the Battle of the Boyne in 1690, thereby establishing Protestant domination of Ireland.

28. Saint Cecilia (d. 230), the patroness of music.

29. William Frend De Morgan (1839–1917), English ceramic artist and novelist, established a pottery business in Chelsea in 1871.

30. *The Imitation of Christ* is usually ascribed to the German religious writer Thomas à Kempis (1380–1471).

31. The English writer and artist William Blake (1757–1827) completed two sets and several miscellaneous drawings illustrating *Paradise Lost* by the English writer John Milton (1608–74). As noted by C. H. Collins Baker in his *Catalogue of William Blake's Drawings and Paintings in the Huntington Library*, 2nd ed., rev. R. R. Wark (San Marino: Huntington Library and Art Gallery, 1957), p. 19, the collection of John Linnell contained a version of the illustration to Book IV generally entitled *Satan Watches Adam and Eve*. Since Yeats had access to the Linnell Collection while preparing *The Works of William Blake* (1893), the allusion here is probably to that particular plate.
   For a color reproduction of another version of the same drawing, see *Paradise Lost*, ed. Philip Hofer and John T. Winterich (New York: Heritage Press, 1940), facing p. 90. The Linnell version is now in the National Gallery, Melbourne.

32. Although the Italian painter Raphael Santi (1483–1520) painted numerous Madonnas, the reference here is presumably to his most famous work, the *Sistine Madonna*.

33. In the Bible, Adam and Eve live in the Garden of Eden until they are banished because of disobedience.

34. This design is reminiscent of a drawing by William Blake captioned "I Want! I Want!", which shows a ladder leaning against the moon and a small figure at the base beginning its climb. The engraving is reproduced in most modern editions, as in *The Poetry and Prose of William Blake*, ed. David V. Erdman (Garden City, N.Y.: Doubleday, 1964), p. 261.

35. Teelin is a tiny fishing-port on the west coast of County Donegal, just north of Donegal Bay.

36. Rathlin Island, off the coast of County Antrim, on the northeast coast of Ireland, would have been the first of the named features of the Irish coast to have been passed on a voyage from Liverpool to Sligo. Tory Island, perhaps 70 miles westward from Rathlin, lies off the coast of County Donegal, on the northwest coast of Ireland. From Tory onward the general trend of the voyage would have been more southerly, to Teelin perhaps 50 miles from Tory, and thence across Donegal Bay more than 20 miles to Sligo.

37. In the Bible, after Adam and Eve are expelled from the Garden

of Eden, God places cherubim and a flaming sword to guard
the entrance.

38. Sheelah Kirby, author of *The Yeats Country*, ed. Patrick Gal-
lagher, 2nd ed. (Dublin: Dolmen, 1963), has suggested that the
house is the old Cummen House in Sligo, some of the ruins of
which can still be seen. As Kirby describes it, Sherman's journey
"seems to have been outward by the lower road, which Yeats
would often have walked with George Pollexfen; then down
from the Cairn by the Primrose Grange side; and home by the
upper road, past Merville, which would bring him along by the
old St. John's Rectory where Mary Carton lived" (letter to
Richard J. Finneran, 20 March 1968).

39. In the Ulster cycle of Irish mythology, Medb (Old Irish, pronounced "Methv"), Medhbh, Maedhbh (Modern Irish, pronounced "Mayv") is represented as queen of the western
province of Connacht and instigator of the war in the epic *Táin
Bó Cuailgne;* she is therefore placed by the pseudo-historians in
the first century A.D. One tradition has her buried in a cairn
on the top of Knocknarea, a mountain near Sligo. The reference
to "sacrifices to the moon" probably derives from a note in
Wood-Martin's *History of Sligo, County and Town:* "Charles
O'Conor, of Blanagar, in one of his unpublished letters, states
the Irish name of the hill to be *Cnoc-na-re,* the hill of the moon,
and he conjectured that it was so called from the ancient inhabitants having performed their Neomenia, or devotions to the
new moon, on the cairn on its summit. By nearly every other
authority this hill is called *Cnoc-na-riagh,* the hill of the execu-
tions" (I: 18n1).

Yeats here accepts the view that Maeve is a source of the
English Mab, queen of the fairies.

EXPLANATORY NOTES TO
DHOYA

1. Although Yeats intends only to place *Dhoya* in the very remote past, he may have been aware that construction of the pyramids in Egypt dates from ca. 2900 B.C.; that the Indian religious leader known as the Buddha was born ca. 563 B.C. and died in 483 B.C.; and that the rise of Japanese painting is usually dated from the introduction of Buddhism in 552. In Germanic mythology, Thor is the Norse god of thunder, might, and war.

2. The Fomorians are demons or evil gods in pagan Irish mythology, converted by the euhemerizing *Book of Invasions* into a race of pirates preying on early settlers of Ireland. Yeats described them in a note in *Poems* (London: T. Fisher Unwin, 1895), p. 283:

> Fomoroh means from under the sea, and is the name of the gods of night and death and cold. The Fomoroh were misshapen and had now the heads of goats and bulls, and now but one leg, and one arm that came out of the middle of their breasts. They were the ancestors of the evil faeries and, according to one Gaelic writer, of all misshapen persons. The giants and the leprecauns are expressly mentioned as of the Fomoroh.

Earlier, in an article in the *Providence Sunday Journal* for 10 February 1889, Yeats termed them a "monstrous race" who "rushed in their pirate galleys century after century like clouds upon the coast." *Letters to the New Island*, ed. George Bornstein and Hugh Witemeyer (New York: Macmillan, 1989), p. 80.

The "Bay of Ballah" is Ballisodare Bay, the southern part of Sligo Bay. As noted by P. W. Joyce in *The Origin and History of Irish Names of Places*, 2nd ed. (Dublin: McGlashan & Gill, 1870), p. 445, "the beautiful rapid on the Owenmore river at Ballysadare in Sligo, has given name to the village. It was originally called *Easdara* (Assdarra), the cataract of the oak; or according to an ancient legend, the cataract of Red Dara, a Fomorian druid who was slain there by Lewy of the long hand. . . . It afterwards took the name of *Baile-easa-Dara*. . . , the town of Dara's cataract, which has been shortened to the present name."

3. In an 1895 note, Yeats summarized the legendary tale of Diarmuid and Grania. Grania was "A beautiful woman, who fled with Dermot to escape from the love of aged Finn. She fled from place to place over Ireland, but at last Dermot was killed at Sligo upon the seaward point of Benbulben, and Finn won her love and brought her, leaning upon his neck, into the assembly of Fenians, who burst into inextinguishable laughter" (*Poems*, p. 283). Yeats is following the version given by Standish Hayes O'Grady, "The Pursuit after Diarmuid O'Duibhne, and Grainne the Daughter of Cormac Mac Airt, King of Ireland in the Third Century," *Transactions of the Ossianic Society*, 3 (1857): 15–211.
In his *History of Sligo, County and Town* (Dublin: Hodges, Figgis, 1882–92), W. G. Wood-Martin describes the "crannoge," or "wooden structure," mentioned in *Dhoya*: "Two crannoges rested on Glencar Lake in olden times. . . . [T]he smaller crannoge is supposed to have been a 'fishing lodge' of the renowned Dermod" (I: 69–70).

4. Ben Bulben and Cope's Mountain are both in County Sligo.

5. In a work which Yeats cites in "Ganconagh's Apology" (see Appendix), Nicholas O'Kearney's translation of "The Festivities at the House of Conan of Ceann-Sleibhe, in the County of Clare," *Transactions of the Ossianic Society*, 2 (1855): 23, Partholan is depicted as a leader of the Fomorians. More usually, however, Partholan is described as an enemy of the Fomorians.

6. In the *History of Sligo, County and Town*, W. G. Wood-Martin describes "a good anchorage called Pooldoy" (III: 221).

7. In an 1898 note, Yeats explains that "The hazel tree was the Irish tree of Life or of Knowledge, and in Ireland it was doubtless, as elsewhere, the tree of the heavens." *The Dome* 1.1 (October 1898): 36.

8. In *Fairy and Folk Tales of the Irish Peasantry* (1888), Yeats explains that "Red is the colour of magic in every country, and has been so from the very earliest times. The caps of fairies and magicians are well-nigh always red." *Prefaces and Introductions*, ed. William H. O'Donnell (New York: Macmillan, 1989), p. 13.

9. Published as "Girl's Song" in *The Wanderings of Oisin and Other Poems* (London: Kegan Paul, Trench & Co., 1889), p. 61. Yeats has made some minor revisions, most notably replacing "ruthless mood" by "evil mood" (l. 5).

10. In *Old Celtic Romances* (London: David Nutt, 1879), P. W. Joyce explains that "Chess-playing was one of the favourite amusements of the ancient Irish chiefs. The game is constantly men-

tioned in the very oldest Gaelic tales; as, for instance, in the 'Cattle-Spoil of Cooley' in 'The Book of the Dun Cow' (A.D. 1100)" (415*n*26). In "The Pursuit after Diarmuid O'Duibhne, and Grainne," O'Grady also indicates that chess was "the favorite game of the Irish in the most ancient times of which we have any account, as appears from the constant mention of it in almost all romantic tales" (144*n*1).

Indeed, a chess game between a mortal and a fairy over a fairy woman occurs in the story of King Eochaid, Edain, and Midhir; as in *Dhoya*, the fairy is triumphant.

11. In the *History of Sligo, County and Town*, Wood-Martin describes "Diarmuid and Grania's bed" as "a natural cavern in the limestone-rock" (I: 70).

12. In "The Pursuit after Diarmuid O'Duibhne, and Grainne," Muadhan describes himself as "a young warrior seeking a lord" (79). Yeats locates his meeting with Diarmuid and Grania in County Sligo, whereas O'Grady places it at the river Lea, "a small rivulet rising to the east of Tralee" (78*n*1), in County Kerry. Also, Muadhan fishes not with a "quicken-berry" but with a "holly berry" according to O'Grady, though he does employ a "straight long rod of a quicken tree" (81).

13. County Donegal is north of County Sligo.

14. Yeats liked to stress the continuity of belief in Irish legendary materials. In a letter to Katharine Tynan in September 1887, for instance, he noted that

I went last Wednesday up Ben Bulban to see the place where Dermot died, a dark pool fabulously deep and still haunted— 1732 feet above the sea line, open to all winds. . . . All peasents at the foot of the mountain know the legend, and know that Dermot still haunts the pool, and fear it. Every hill and stream is some way or other connected with the story.

The Collected Letters of W. B. Yeats: Volume One, 1865–1895, ed. John Kelly (Oxford: Clarendon Press, 1986), p. 37.

EXPLANATORY NOTE TO "GANCONAGH'S APOLOGY"

1. In his translation of "The Festivities at the House of Conan of Ceann-Sleibhe, in the County of Clare," *Transactions of the Ossianic Society*, 2 (1855): 18–19, Nicholas O'Kearney defines a "Ganconagh" as follows: "The Gean-cānach (love-talker) was another diminutive being of the same tribe, but, unlike the Luchryman, he personated love and idleness, and always appeared with a dudeen in his jaw in lonesome valleys, and it was his custom to make love to shepherdesses and milkmaids: it was considered very unlucky to meet him; and whoever was known to have ruined his fortune by devotion to the fair sex was said to have met a Geancanach. The dudeen, or ancient Irish tobacco pipe found in our rathes, &c., is still popularly called a Geancanach's pipe." This definition is quoted in *Fairy and Folk Tales of the Irish Peasantry* (1888) in a note on the Geancanach attributed to Douglas Hyde. A shorter version of O'Kearney's commentary is also included in *Irish Fairy Tales* (1892), where the Geancanach is included in the list of "The Solitary Fairies." See W. B. Yeats, *Prefaces and Introductions*, ed. William H. O'Donnell (New York: Macmillan, 1989), pp. 63, 196–97.

Printed in the United States
By Bookmasters